FINDING REFUGE
BOOK 2 OF THE MARKED ONES
by Cathi Shaw

Ink Smith Publishing
www.ink-smith.com

Finding Refuge
Book 2 of the Marked Ones
By Cathi Shaw

Copyright 2014 by Cathi Shaw

Cover Design: Chris Arlidge of Cheeky Monkey Media
Map by Linda Bjarnason
Author Photo by Becca McNeil
(http://www.beccamcneilphotography.com/)

ISBN: 978-1-939156-61-7
Ink Smith Publishing
P.O. Box Box 1086
Glendora CA
www.inksmith.com

Table of Contents

ACKNOWLEDGEMENTS

There are so many people to thank for making *Finding Refuge* a reality. First and foremost, I would like to thank all the people who read *Five Corners: Book 1 of the Marked Ones*. Your feedback and enthusiasm for more inspired me so much.

Once again I've been blessed with an incredible group of beta readers for this book.
Thanks to: Caitie Shaw, Dan Nixon, Wendy Nixon, Kate Fitzsimmons, Mackenzie Nelson, and Carol Doyle-Jones.

Thank you to everyone at Cheeky Monkey Media (http://cheekymonkeymedia.ca/) for the amazing vision you had of transferring my stories to illustrations and the web. Special thanks to Treena Bjarnason and Chris Arlidge, whose professionalism and talent continue to astound me!

Big thanks, of course, to my family and friends who were incredibly supportive of my work on Finding Refuge. Your positive energy continues to be a great treasure to me.

DEDICATION

For Dr. Muriel Edith Shaw, the strongest woman I've ever had the
privilege of knowing and loving.
I miss you more than words can express! Ox

CHAPTER ONE

Kiara's lungs burned as she ran through the dusty landscape, her arms aching with the weight of the small child she clutched to her chest.

"Shhhh," Kiara hissed as the child whimpered, the noise carrying over the rocky terrain. She glanced over her shoulder, looking for signs of pursuit. In the distance she could just barely make out the black blur that indicated a Hunter was there. One at least. She kept running. There was no time to see if there were more.

The Hunters had sniffed this child out just as Kiara had talked the mother into releasing her into Kiara's care. Kiara had heard the Hunter's telltale hiss and had begun to run. Oddly enough the Hunter hadn't teleported. But Kiara didn't have time to dwell on the possible reasons for that. She had to get back to the camp in the mountains and she knew she wouldn't make it taking the more travelled road.

"Mama!" The girl in her arms wailed miserably.

"Hush!" Kiara panted, squeezing the child tightly, which only resulted in an escalating howl of rage from her small passenger. Caedmon was so much better at this than she was. Despite his size and the rough manners he'd honed from his years in the army, Caedmon was surprisingly gentle with the children. They felt instantly safe in his arms. Kiara had to admit that she understood the feeling. Although it had been months now since she'd been alone with Caedmon, he still made her feel safe.

She stumbled on a rock and almost went down, jerking her thoughts back to the task at hand. She didn't risk another look over her shoulder but knew the Hunter was gaining on her. It had to be, they moved faster than she could even at the best of times and the child in her arms was not cooperating as she continued to wail at an increasing frequency.

Looking ahead she saw a steep path winding up the side of the mountain. She had no choice; she would have to leave the main road and climb. If her luck held, she would stay ahead of the Hunter. Hidden within the hills lay Caedmon and safety.

As she forced her legs forward, Kiara cursed her impatience. She should have waited for Caedmon to come with her to the small village. He was going to be furious at her for risking so much. But if she had done that the girl in her arms would very likely be dead by now, she reminded herself. She had rescued her just barely in time.

They had been seeking out the Marked children all summer. They had already ferried two groups of children to Bellasiel in the Eastern Mountains but they'd also found dozens of Marked Ones slain. Kiara was determined to save as many of the remaining children as she could before winter set in. Right now they had the largest group of Marked children they'd collected yet - more than twenty of them. And Caedmon was getting nervous.

It was dangerous traveling with the children, as they'd soon learned. But it was more so with the group they currently had because it was so large. They were sure to draw attention if they went into villages. They couldn't stay in proper shelters. The network of sympathizers for the Marked Ones, known as Helpers, was growing across the Five Corners but they had to be sure they could trust the Helpers with their lives before they would stay with them. Bellasiel was reluctant to sanction such actions yet. She hoped by next summer they would have a number of safe houses to take the children they found. But for now they were stuck with camping in remote locations - less than ideal conditions when they were traveling with children as young as two years old.

Suddenly the girl in her arms twisted and wriggled violently. Kiara clutched her closer but lost her footing and they both fell hard at the top of the steep incline. The child began to scream and before Kiara could do anything she heard the sibilant voice of the Hunter.

"Give me the child."

Kiara pushed herself to sitting, tucking the now silent girl behind her. "No," she said firmly, forcing herself to make eye contact with the vile creature in front of her.

The Hunter's hood was pulled low but she could still see the eerie glow from its red eyes. She knew that beneath the dark robes lay a creature with skin as translucent as glass, its blue veins clearly visible. The idyll thought that sun would not be kind to such skin floated through her mind.

"Fine," the creature almost shrugged, "I will take you first."

It advanced toward Kiara. She reached for her sword before remembering that she'd left it at the camp. A broadsword, even one crafted in Séreméla, was far too heavy to carry on a rescue mission. She reached for the dagger in her boot but it was too late. The Hunter moved with a speed that would have been shocking if Kiara hadn't seen it before. As its gloved hand closed around her throat, Kiara forced herself to look into its eyes, where she saw all hope for the Marked Ones being devoured.

Spots clouded her vision and Kiara felt a searing heat radiating from where the Hunter grasped her throat. She watched as the blackness reflected in the red eyes turned to pure white energy. As darkness began closing in on the edges of her vision, she could see the Hunter's eyes, feasting on whatever it saw in her own eyes.

"You never had a chance at saving them. You should have saved yourself," it hissed softly as the blackness began to overtake her.

Suddenly Kiara found herself on the ground, her vision still dark. She heard the screaming hiss that announced the death of a Hunter, then she felt herself being lifted by familiar strong arms. Caedmon, was her last thought before she slipped under the blackness.

#

It was late afternoon when Kiara woke. She was lying on a makeshift cot near the fire in the camp. Caedmon was sitting next to her, watching her. His expression was just short of thunderous.

"The child?" Kiara asked and was surprised when her voice came out hoarse.

Caedmon didn't answer for a moment. Then he jerked his dark head toward the other side of the camp. Ignoring the pain in her neck, Kiara forced herself to turn in the direction he'd indicated. She saw the little girl playing happily with one of the older children and relief flooded her.

"She made it."

"You almost didn't," Caedmon growled angrily.

No, he was more than angry. Kiara took a deep breath, searching for words. But Caedmon didn't let her speak.

"Don't bother, Kiara. This isn't a game."

"I know it's not a game," she responded sharply, despite her guilt.

"Do you? Because you seem to be upping the stakes more and more lately. Taking unnecessary chances. Going off to fetch that child on your own, when we knew the Hunters were not far behind us. Nevermind the risks we are taking by traveling with this many children!"

He stood and began to pace, his large frame vibrating with rage.

"Caedmon," Kiara whispered, her heart twisting.

He turned suddenly. "Do you even see what you're doing, Kiara? You've become like one of them. You're addicted to the hunt!"

Hot tears pricked at Kiara's eyes. "I am not like a Hunter," she denied as anger swelled inside her.

"Yes. You are." Caedmon stopped pacing and crouched down beside her. "You are. You may not hunt for the same reasons but you are drawn to do this. At all odds. Do you think you've achieved what you set out to?" He gestured toward the children in the camp. "Just because you've got them here doesn't mean we'll make it to the Refuge with them all."

Reluctantly, Kiara looked around the camp. She knew Caedmon was right. They had to get these children to Bellasiel but what about all the others they would be leaving to sure death. She couldn't bear the thought of more dead children.

"We can find more."

"No!" Caedmon roared, his handsome face twisted in anger. "Kiara, we can't find more. We will *all* die if we try to." He paused when he saw the look on her face. Then he softened, "I know you want to help as many of these children as you can. But the Hunters are on our trail. You almost died today. You know as well as I do that the Hunters are increasing in number. And they've had no trouble sniffing us out. The time has come to focus on getting these children back to the Refuge."

Kiara closed her eyes. In her heart she knew he was right but the appearance of the Hunters meant sure death to so many more.

"Kee, you have to let it go. We can't save them all. We can only do our best."

Tears pricked at her eyes as Kiara looked across the camp at the groups of children playing softly. It wasn't fair that these children had to run for their lives. They should be allowed to live as children not as refugees, torn away from their families.

She felt Caedmon's strong fingers stroking her cheek.

"Loving you will be the death of me," he whispered, almost too softly for her to hear.

She looked at Caedmon and saw the raw hurt on his face. Kiara's chest tightened. She never wanted to hurt Caedmon.

"Do you have any idea what it was like to find you like that?" he asked quietly. "I thought you were dead." His voice broke and he stood abruptly. She watched as he turned away from her. Caedmon was never one to show his emotions. He saw it as a sign of weakness. The fact that he was showing her such a depth of emotion now just served to show how much she was hurting him. Kiara felt the tears that had been threatening earlier suddenly hot on her cheeks.

"We'll break camp at first light." Caedmon said over his shoulder before he strode across the camp, leaving her lying by the fire.

Kiara brushed the tears away and focused on his words. They both knew it was at least a two-week journey to the Refuge in the Eastern Mountains.

She looked over at the children playing happily in the camp and closed her eyes. She just hoped they could make it.

CHAPTER TWO

The tingling began in her fingertips. Thia took a deep breath and slowly let it out, holding the vibrating energy at bay. The tingling grew more insistent and Thia felt the threat of a seizure creeping up her arms. She focused more keenly on her breathing, reminding herself that she was in control. Despite her eyes being closed, colors collided beneath her eyelids and then she was pulled from her meditation into a vision.

Teague beaten and bruised hanging in chains from a damp, stone wall. Teague's fingers closing around her neck and choking the very life from her. Teague's silver eyes turning cold and hard as hatred filled them.

Abruptly Thia jerked herself from the vision. She opened her eyes to find herself lying on the floor, her breath coming in gasps as the visions slowly faded from her mind. After a moment she sat up and brushed her cheeks to find them wet with tears. She didn't want to think about what the visions might mean.

Thia forced herself to her feet. Dizziness and fatigue swept over her but she crossed the small room to stand at the window. Just outside was one of the busiest streets of Sailsburg. Her head throbbed as she absently pressed her fingers to her temples and thought about the previous night's dreamwalk. She couldn't shake the unease that was filling her. First the dreamwalk and then the vision.

There was something about Teague that wasn't right. Thia tried to remember precisely what had been different about the dreamwalk but as she pushed herself to call forth the memory the pain in her head intensified for a few moments. She gasped as she let the mental probing slip away.

It had been months since she'd seen Teague in person and she was becoming increasingly concerned by what he was telling her in their dreamwalks.

Teague had gone with Kiara and Caedmon to the Eastern Mountains. The urgency to get him there and out of grasp of the *Draíodóir* had been strong. The *Draíodóir* were a mysterious sect of Druids who were greatly feared in the Five Corners. Little was known about them because they didn't mingle with outsiders and almost no one left their numbers. They were desperate to keep Teague in their grasp. Bellasiel, the Elder healer, had promised that there was someone at the safe haven in the Eastern Mountains who could help Teague. A former *Draíodóir* apprentice who could help to break the ties the sect had on Teague's mind. And at first it had seemed as if the man had actually been helpful. But now Thia was starting to wonder.

But, to be honest, she really couldn't judge just how well Teague was doing when she was so far away from him. She had only their dreamwalks through which to gauge his mood and dream emotions were sketchy at the best of times. What she really needed was to go to the Eastern Mountains herself and see Teague in person. She was certain she could help him. And the vision she'd just experienced only intensified that feeling.

Thia absently heard the door behind her open. She turned as her sister, Mina, came in. Mina was looking excited and happy, her green eyes dancing with light. But her expression sobered when she saw Thia.

"You're not going to hide in the room again all day, are you?" she asked, disappointment and worry tingeing her words. Thia knew that Mina was loving every minute of their travels. She saw it all as a great adventure – one she'd been waiting her entire life for. Mina certainly showed no sign of wanting to turn toward the East.

Thia turned back to the window and looked out at the crowded streets of Sailsburg in front of her. It was the most Southern port in the Five Corners and she didn't like it. Besides the crowds of strangely dressed people, she didn't enjoy the hot salty ocean scented air. It made her long for the cool forests of home.

But Mina appeared to thrive on it.

"Please, Thia, come out and explore with me."

Thia turned to her sister. "Mina, when are we going to move to the East?" she asked seriously.

Mina paused. "I don't know," she admitted, looking sheepish. "Meldiron is determined to find Arion. He feels we are close to finding him here. He has had several promising leads."

Thia shook her head impatiently. "He had those leads weeks ago and so far nothing has panned out from them." Her thoughts returned to Teague. "I wish we'd start on the journey to the mountains."

Mina's smile faded. "Why? Has something happened?"

Thia sighed and closed her eyes. "Nothing concrete but, Mina, I can't shake the feeling that something is wrong with Teague. And you know what it would mean if the *Draíodóir* were able to reinforce their connection with him."

Mina nodded, a worried expression creasing her pretty face. "The Refuge would be in danger."

Thia nodded miserably. She didn't want to share her vision with her sister. Sometimes what she saw actually came to be and many times it just didn't make any sense. She was hoping that the disturbing images of Teague were her mind's way of urging her to turn East. She decided to focus on what she'd discovered in the dreamwalks.

"I don't want it to be true but Teague has been acting differently. I can't explain it," she gestured in frustration, "The dreamwalks are not the best form of communication. But I know something is wrong. Can you try speaking to Meldiron?"

Mina nodded. "I will. Are you sure you don't want to come with me? It might do you some good to get some fresh air."

Thia looked at the crowded streets again and shuddered. "Very sure."

"Okay." Mina turned to door but she paused before stepping through it. "Thia, try not to worry. I'm sure it will be well."

Thia watched her sister leave and wished she could feel the same unerring optimism as Mina did. But she couldn't shake the images from her vision out of her mind. She feared the worse.

#

Mina found Meldiron not far from the Inn. She told him of Thia's worries but he shrugged it off. Mina felt a prick of irritation. Her brother was a good man but he had a touch of arrogance that annoyed her at times. She suspected it came from being raised as an Elder prince.

"Thia is just restless. And I don't blame her," he brushed off her sister's concerns easily as he scanned the street, his green eyes ever seeking. "But we are so close to finding Arion, we can't leave now."

Mina looked at her brother in concern. His desire to find Arion, his closest kinsman, was understandable but she was starting to worry that he had developed an obsession. And, in her experience, obsessions rarely led to clear thinking.

"How do you know we are close to finding him, Meldiron? We've been here for three weeks with no new leads." She reached out and grabbed his arm when she saw his attention was flagging. "Meldiron." He looked at her. "Do you have new information?"

She saw despair flash briefly in his eyes. "Nothing concrete," he admitted softly. "But, Mina, we are close to finding him. I can feel it here." He pounded his chest.

Mina looked at him doubtfully. She didn't think her little sister was going to be swayed by a feeling in Meldiron's heart. Mina took a deep breath and blew it out as she followed her brother through the streets of Sailsburg. Meldiron, crown prince of the Elder people, was used to getting his way. And on this journey with him she'd learned that he was more stubborn than even Kiara.

She also found herself playing the role of referee more and more between Thia and him. While Meldiron was her brother by birth, she had grown up with Thia and she was more her sibling than any blood ties could secure. But Mina loved them both and having to constantly mediate their disagreements was exhausting.

Thia had changed since she returned with Teague last spring. Her sister had spent time underground with The People, a group of beings who had removed themselves from the surface centuries ago. And while there Thia had learned that both her and Teague were the offspring of an ill-fated coupling between The People and the surface dwellers. There were a handful of halflings like them, most of them dead.

Yes, Thia's trip to the Underground had changed her. She had become more short-tempered than she'd ever been in her life. And since they'd arrived at Sailsburg, she'd become even more agitated. Mina feared that her sister would begin the journey East with or without them soon. And it wasn't safe for any of the Marked Ones to travel on their own but especially Thia with her tendency toward seizures.

Meldiron had stopped just ahead of Mina and was conversing with the owner of a bakery. The man was nodding vigorously and pointing down the street.

Meldiron thanked him and turned to Mina. "He's seen Arion."

Mina looked at her brother skeptically. This wasn't the first time Meldiron had insisted Arion had been spotted. "Are you sure?" she asked, doubt tingeing her words.

Meldiron nodded then paused. For a moment defeat darkened his features. He looked down at Mina, pleadingly. "It won't hurt to find out, will it? What's the worse that can happen? Another dead end?"

Arion had been like a brother to Meldiron as they grew up in Séreméla. The fact that he had been the one to send Arion off on a potentially deadly expedition was eating at Meldiron. Mina knew her brother felt immense guilt at the thought that Arion might have been killed. He needed some kind of closure to move on.

Relenting Mina gestured for him to continue. Truthfully it wasn't a dead end she was worried about but Meldiron's disappointment if it turned out to be another false lead. She knew her brother felt responsible for Arion's fate. He, after all, was the one who had sent his kinsman on this journey and he'd done so to protect Mina and her sisters. If Arion was dead, he would blame himself.

They threaded their way through the crowded streets until they came to a small novelty shop.

"The baker said that someone who matches Arion's description has taken a room above the shop," Meldiron explained.

Mina looked at the shop dubiously noting the peeling paint on the building and the shutters hanging at odd angles. There were rough looking men and desperate looking women crowding the streets as they pushed their way past. If Arion wasn't the person renting the room above the store, Mina expected that whoever was renting the room would not be too pleased to see them. But she held her tongue and followed Meldiron up the narrow stairwell.

The stairs were steep and reeked of days old urine. Mina wrinkled her nose. Arion, who was used to living in the Sanctuary with the crown prince of the Elders, had certainly sunk low if these were, indeed, his lodgings.

Meldiron paused at the top of the stairs and looked over his shoulder at her.

"What are you waiting for?" Mina asked.

He smiled sadly. "I don't know. I'm just ..." he closed his eyes. "If this isn't Arion, I'm afraid you're right Mina. We've exhausted all possible avenues of his safe escape. If he isn't here, then I'll have to admit defeat. If this turns out to not be Arion, then we'll leave tomorrow for the Eastern Mountains."

Mina's heart twisted when she saw the anguish on her brother's features. She knew what it cost him to admit defeat. Suddenly she hoped with all her heart that his friend was behind that door.

"Go on," she urged.

Meldiron nodded, took a deep breath and knocked on the door.

They could hear a scrambling on the other side of the door. Meldiron reached for the dagger at his belt. Mina did the same. If this was not Arion then it was possible that they would be attacked.

When the door still did not open, Meldiron knocked again and spoke loudly in the Elder language.

Suddenly the door burst open to reveal a tall dark haired Elder. "Dearthair?" he breathed.

Meldiron let out a laugh and suddenly the two men were embracing. Mina stood in the hallway awkwardly, feeling like she was intruding on a private moment.

"How did you find me?" Arion asked, disbelief clear in his voice. He was taller even than Meldiron. Mina couldn't help staring as he was the only dark haired Elder she'd ever seen. And yet his features were clearly Elder. He was not as handsome as her brother and yet he was somehow more ruggedly beautiful. And his eyes were such a light green, so different than the dark green that both Meldiron and herself possessed, that she couldn't pull her gaze away from them.

"I'm stubborn," Meldiron said with a grin.

Arion seemed to recollect himself. "Come in, come in." As Meldiron stepped forward Arion's gaze fell on Mina.

"You are not alone?" he said, his voice suddenly cold.

Meldiron suddenly remembered himself. "Arion, you've met Minathrial before."

"Princess," he breathed, his eyes locking with her own and Mina had to stop herself from recoiling at the hostility that was reflected in those pale green depths. "Forgive me, I didn't recognize you. You've recovered." Despite the fact that the words were positive, Mina couldn't miss Arion's dark tone. Had he hoped she wouldn't recover?

Meldiron didn't seem to notice. He laughed and pulled Mina into the room past Arion. "She's recovered completely."

"I'm sorry but have we met?" Mina asked, confused.

"Arion was with the party that came to the Inn, Mina. He saw you when you were sick."

Mina nodded. She still had no recollection of that time. Arion continued to stare at her, his gaze very intense. Mina looked at the filthy floor and felt her cheeks heat.

Finally Arion turned to Meldiron and she couldn't help noticing the puckering of the skin on his neck just above his tunic collar. She remembered the story her brother had told her about Arion. How his own mother had tried to burn the Mark from his shoulder by using acid and how he had almost died as a result. While his life had been saved, Meldiron had said that his friend's back and chest had been disfigured for life.

Mina tried to imagine a mother doing such a thing to her own child. Pity for the dark-haired boy who had endured such abuse filled her. His hostility was perhaps understandable. She felt herself softening towards him. Arion suddenly looked at her and, as if he could read her thoughts, his gaze hardened.

Mina looked down again, embarrassed.

"We have much to tell you," Meldiron said.

"And I have much to share with you," Arion returned darkly. "I fear you've put yourselves in even more danger by coming here, my friend."

Finding Refuge

CHAPTER THREE

Meldiron insisted on taking Arion back to their lodgings in a safer part of the city. After securing him a room, they met in the common area for the evening meal.

Meldiron brought Arion up to speed on what had happened in Séreméla causing them to flee. Arion was clearly stunned by the news that the wards, which had guarded the city for years, had come down and the extent of the corruption that had been revealed about the Council of Elders.

When Meldiron recounted how his own men had attacked him and left him for dead, Mina noticed Arion's fingers tighten until his knuckles were white. But he did not look surprised when Meldiron told him that Bellasiel had helped them and even had a safe place for them to hide until they knew whom they could trust.

"I told you Bellasiel had a good heart," Meldiron said.

"She was deeply engrained in the Council doings, Meldiron. You can't blame me for doubting her loyalties. Not after all that has happened."

Meldiron nodded reluctantly and Mina couldn't help wondering exactly what the Council had been involved in that Meldiron had not shared with her. But her brother changed the topic swiftly.

"Enough talk of Séreméla for one night. Tell me what has happened to you, my friend?" Meldiron asked after they finished dinner.

Mina leaned forward. She knew that Arion had been part of a decoy team of four Elders sent South to keep the Hunters off their tracks. But they didn't know what had happened to those decoy teams. Meldiron had feared the worse and that was one of the reasons for his obsession in trying to find Arion. He couldn't bear the thought that he may have sent his friend, who also bore the Mark, to certain death.

But Arion's mother had unknowingly given him the one thing that had protected him. When he'd been only three years old, his mother had tried to remove his Mark forever by dousing her small son in acid. That horrific act had almost killed him and had resulted in the disfiguring scars across his back, shoulders and chest. While it had not killed Arion, it had achieved his mother's goal. Meldiron had told Mina that Arion's Mark was hidden under the thick scar tissue.

As a result of this scarring, no one in Séreméla knew that Arion was Marked. This had likely protected him from attack on his journey South. But Meldiron had worried nevertheless. As he pointed out, it appeared that the Hunters didn't find their victims by seeing the Mark. He thought they might sniff it out.

A bitter smile twisted Arion's lips when he heard Meldiron's theory. "You might be right about that," he said. "It would explain what happened to our decoy party."

Arion explained that after they had left the others at the Inn, they had galloped South for several days. There had been no sign of pursuit and the closer they got to Sailsburg the more Arion had feared that the decoying hadn't worked. Then suddenly they had been attacked. And not by just one Hunter, but three!

"Three Hunters had felt capable of taking on four Elders?" Meldiron asked after a moment of stunned silence.

Arion nodded. "Obviously they wanted what we had very much. We killed two of them but lost two of our own party in the battle." He fell silent, remembering his kinsmen. Meldiron also looked somber.

Thia spoke up suddenly, "What happened to the last Hunter?"

Arion furrowed his brow. "That was what was so strange. It found the blood and was not happy. But then it sniffed the air and looked straight at me. It was as if it *knew* what I was. Then it attacked me. It was outnumbered and we were able to kill it easily. But I always wondered what the sniffing was about. I wonder now, Meldiron, if you're not right about their abilities. Perhaps that's why they are being hired as assassins."

Mina frowned. "But who is hiring them and where are they finding such creatures?"

Arion look directly at her and Mina felt an inexplicable shiver of excitement curl in her stomach. He was so intense. For a moment she was so overcome by the sensation that she didn't notice his lips were moving.

"They are not creatures, Princess Minathrial," he was saying. "They are men. A strange sort of men, I will agree, but they are very real. They come from an island in the ocean to the southwest of here." He laughed bitterly. "They even freely trade with the merchants in Sailsburg."

"How is that possible?" Meldiron demanded. "Don't they know what these people are capable of?"

Arion nodded grimly. "Of course they do. You don't imagine that the Marked Ones are the only targets of the Nasseet assassins, do you? Over the centuries they have been considered the most deadly of killers. But they also are able to trade things that are not available in the Five Corners. And, despite their killing ways, they appear to be honest traders. The Sailsburg merchants have an uneasy truce with the Nasseet traders. But as long as the merchants are honest in their dealings they have no problems."

"And the ones that aren't honest?" Meldiron asked grimly.

"They end up dead."

"Now that we've found Arion," Thia suddenly interrupted. Mina turned to her sister in surprise. It was completely out of character for little Thia to say anything during their meetings. Or at least it had been until recently. Lately she had been far more outspoken than usual, even exchanging words with Meldiron that bordered on arguments. The Elders paused in their dialogue and turned to Thia.

Thia looked at them steadily. "Are we able to continue on to the Eastern Mountains?"

Mina looked at her sister. She'd been largely quiet during the discussion but her face was worried and pinched and she'd hardly eaten any of her food.

Meldiron shook his head. "I'd like to delay returning just yet," he mused. "It would be interesting to see the land the Nasseet come from. Do you think we could obtain passage there?" he asked Arion.

Mina felt a jolt of excitement mixed with fear race through her. A trip to the island where the Hunters lived … while going outside Five Corners was appealing to her travelling soul, the thought of encountering even one Hunter, nevermind an island full of them, filled her with terror. While she had no clear memory of the Hunter attack she'd just barely survived, the mere talk of the creatures filled her with a sense of dread she didn't understand.

Arion studied Meldiron, clearly weighing the possibility of an expedition to Nasseet. "It will be difficult," he admitted. "We could canvass the sailors in the port but the easiest way to get to Nasseet is going to be stowing away on one of their vessels."

Mina listened as the men began discussing different scenarios for obtaining passage South. A sick feeling began to grow in her stomach.

Suddenly there was a crash at the end of the table. They all turned to see Thia on her feet, her golden eyes blazing with anger, her fiery curls a halo around her head. She looked truly fearsome, despite her tiny stature.

"You will listen to me, Meldiron. Extending our adventure to the mystical land of Nasseet was not part of the plan. We were to return to the Eastern Mountains months ago but your obsession with finding Arion delayed us." She paused and looked at Arion. "We have found him now but I won't tell you again that it is imperative that we return to the Eastern Mountains as soon as possible and I will not be ignored."

Meldiron's face was serious as he observed Thia's rage. "What has happened?" he asked solemnly.

Thia's face suddenly crumbled, all fire and light going out of her as tears filled her eyes. "I fear we may be losing Teague."

#

Thia's revelation quickly convinced all of them that the journey East must not been delayed.

Mina listened as her sister explained her fears.

"Teague has been growing more and more agitated in our dreamwalks," Thia admitted. "At first I thought it was just our delay that was troubling him, but he seems to be growing almost …" she paused before reluctantly continuing "…paranoid."

Arion eyes narrowed. "Paranoid in what way?"

"He doesn't trust Bellasiel or the former *Draíodóir* who is working with him. He told me he thinks they have greater plans and that the Marked Ones are just pawns in their bid for power." She frowned. "How much do you trust Bellasiel, Meldiron?"

Mina's brother answered immediately, "Bellesiel is trustworthy. But that doesn't mean that her wish for justice couldn't have certain … quirks to it. I don't believe she would harm any of the Marked Ones, though."

"There's more," Thia said. "Lately Teague has been saying that he doesn't trust Caedmon and Kiara. He says that they've bought into Bellesiel's plan and are her sentries. They've brought thirty-five Marked children to the Refuge this summer and are currently on a mission to find more." Thia paused. "But his talk of Caedmon is laced with bitterness and almost … hatred." She looked at each of them, worry clear in her golden eyes.

Mina gasped. Teague and his adopted brother were close. She couldn't imagine him ever turning against Caedmon. In fact, she could hardly believe Teague would turn against anyone. He was a happy-go-lucky sweet boy. And a gifted musician. She remembered what fun they had had playing songs together the previous year. It was hard to imagine an angry or bitter Teague. It just didn't seem to be in his character to say a bad thing about anyone. Suddenly she was just as worried as Thia.

Thia nodded. "Something is happening to Teague. He was angry with me last time I dreamwalked with him." Her voice caught and she paused for a moment before adding softly, "And that has never happened before."

Meldiron's green eyes were serious. "We'll start our trip to the Eastern Mountains at first light. We may have delayed too long."

They sat in silence for a while, then Arion and Meldiron began discussing the swiftest route East. She was amazed at how quickly they could shift their focus. One moment they were planning a secret expedition to Nasseet and the next they were deciding the fastest route eastward. Mina sat and listened to her brother and Arion plan out the trip in detail. But before they retired for the night another thought occurred to her.

"Arion?" she said quietly. They stopped talking and looked at her. "What happened to your kinsman? The only survivor of the attack besides you."

A kind of shutter seemed to drop over Arion's face. "He disappeared three weeks ago," he answered evasively.

Meldiron looked concerned. "Do you think he was contacted by the Elder council?"

Arion shook his head dismissively. "I'm not sure."

Meldiron shrugged and returned to the map they'd been pouring over.

Mina continued to watch Arion though. Something told her he knew what had happened to the missing Elder but he wasn't going to tell them – at least not yet.

He must have felt her watching him because Arion looked up and met her eyes. She shivered when she saw how cold the expression was in the pale green depths of his eyes.

Mina excused herself to retire for the evening a short time later. Thia had already gone to their room to pack up her belongings. But as Mina was about to mount the stairs, a strong hand closed over her wrist and pulled her into an alcove below the stairs.

Mina gasped when she saw it was Arion.

"Leave the questions alone, Princess," he said menacingly. "Meldiron doesn't need to know the answers."

Mina stared at him, shocked to see that his handsome face was cruel.

"Do you know how long and hard my brother has been searching for you?" she asked in disbelief.

"Your brother must be protected," he said savagely. "Don't ask questions that will only end up causing him pain."

With that he released her and bounded past her up the stairs.

Mina rubbed her wrist and watched him go, wondering what he meant. How could what he knew cause Meldiron pain? It was a question that she intended to uncover the answer to.

CHAPTER FOUR

They left Sailsburg as the sun crept over the sails in the harbor the next morning. A wave of excitement crested over Mina as they guided their horses along the road out of town. To travel the Five Corners had been her lifelong dream and now it was coming true, even if it was under less than ideal circumstances.

Mina's excitement dampened at bit when she caught sight of her sister's pinched face. Thia, who hated riding, had not complained as they'd mounted their horses. It was a testament to how desperate she was to reach Teague. Mina hoped the journey would prove swift and uneventful for Thia's sake. She had noticed that her sister hadn't slept for most of the night and couldn't help wondering if it was because she didn't want to encounter Teague in a dream. While Thia had been close lipped about what had actually happened in her last dreamwalk with Teague, Mina sensed there was more her sister was keeping to herself about their friend.

Sailsburg had a number of roads into town - one from the West, one from the North and one from the East. When they arrived on the coast almost a month go, they had entered the coastal city by the Northern gate, now they were leaving it along the Eastern road and Mina was stunned by the difference in landscape.

She remembered from the maps that Arion and Meldiron had consulted the night before that the Eastern road followed the sea for about a hundred kilometers before it turned inland and took a North Eastern passage. Mina looked out at the cerulean water that was dancing and sparkling to her right and filled her lungs with a deep breathe of the fresh salty air.

She couldn't help wondering what they would find in the Eastern part of their country. So far she had been extremely surprised by the differences in the terrain in the different places she'd traveled. Her home in the Lowlands was all lush, green forests, Séreméla was a tropical paradise, although she didn't know how much of that was due to magik or naturally occurring. And Sailsburg was a warm idyllic city by the sea.

Finding Refuge

As they left the outskirts of the city, Mina was stunned by the great sand dunes that rose by the road. She'd never seen anything like them and she wondered how far the dunes extended. They seemed vast.

When she said as much to Meldiron, he nodded. "They are amazingly extensive; however, they are dying."

Mina looked at him incredulously unable to believe that such magnificent landforms could be in danger of disappearing.

"It's true." Her brother told her when he saw the skepticism on her face. "They used to stretch much further inland but over the years the sea takes a bit of them back."

Mina stared at the sparkling ocean as it gently lapped at the shore and wondered how it could devour something as vast as the dunes. Clearly the sea had more mysteries than she realized.

They continued along the road until mid-day when they halted for a meal. Mina was thrilled when Meldiron led them off the road into the dunes, just far enough that they wouldn't be spotted. Although there was no indication that they were being pursued, travelling this close to the harbor that freely traded with Nasseet meant they had to take precautions.

She dismounted and knelt to run her fingers through the sand that made up the dunes. It was fine and silky, slipping through her fingers and being caught up easily by the light breeze that was blowing. What an amazing place this was.

"Mina, come on, we don't have all day to sightsee. Let's have our lunch and get back on the road." Meldiron called to her.

Reluctantly Mina joined the others. It was really her only complaint about travelling with her brother – he never let her stay long enough in one place to really soak up her surroundings.

They had just settled down on a small sand dune when they heard a strange cry.

"What was that?" Meldiron asked Arion. He shrugged indicating he didn't know.

"Was it a bird?" Mina asked.

Thia shook her head. "It sounded like someone in pain."

Meldiron and Arion looked at one another and stood. The sound came again and they starting in the direction of the noise, their hands on their swords.

Mina scrambled to her feet and followed them as they edged further into the dunes. She almost crashed into Arion when they abruptly stopped. The dark Elder glared at her over his shoulder. Mina stood on her tiptoes to see what they were blocking from her view.

Lying on the sand there was the most pitiful creature Mina had ever seen. With translucent skin, a hairless head and red weeping eyes, it was clearly a girl from Nasseet. She was naked. But Mina had never seen a Hunter in such distress.

Lying uncovered in the sun, her thin skin had blistered and begun to weep. It looked almost as though she'd been dumped here to die. At first, Mina couldn't tell if the girl was conscious but as Meldiron stepped closer she flinched and that strange cry escaped her lips again.

Arion pulled his sword from his scabbard.

"No!" Mina said stepping in front of him, unable to believe that he would kill so easily.

"We don't know why it's here, we have to assume it is a threat," he said coldly. "Get out of my way, Princess Minathrial."

But to Mina's relief, Meldiron gave his kinsman a hard look. "Don't be ridiculous, Arion, she is hardly a threat." He removed his shirt and covered the poor girl with it, to shield her skin from the burning sun.

Mina winced when she saw sand crusted in her thin skin.

"I'll get Thia," she said, turning and running back to where her sister was resting with the horses.

Thia was a gifted healer and she was going to need all her skill to help the Nasseet girl. Mina quickly explained what they'd found and Thia was on her feet in seconds. Mina grabbed Thia's bag and they hurried back to where the girl was lying. She was unconscious when they returned but Meldiron was sitting near her in the sand. Mina noticed that Arion had stalked off to the far side of the dune and was looking broodingly over the ocean.

Thia didn't speak but went right to work assessing the girl.

"Will she live?" Meldiron asked and Mina was surprised to hear the anguish in her brother's voice. He was trained as a soldier, she didn't expect him to be so affected by suffering.

Thia did not reply right away. "We need to get her off this hot sand. Mina, there's a blanket in my bag, can you grab it?"

When Mina had spread the blanket on the sand, Thia motioned for Meldiron to lift the now unconscious girl onto it. As the extent of her injuries were exposed, Mina cringed. Much of her fragile skin seemed to have blistered so badly the flesh beneath was exposed. Thia shook her head and then dug through her bag.

She pulled out a variety of jars of salve and herbs and began covering the girl's skin with the medicines in them. After she had finished, Thia carefully bandaged the injuries with linen and then she looked up.

"We need to get some liquid in her. The burns are only one thing, she is also severely dehydrated."

Mina reached into the bag and pulled out her canteen.

Thia took it and held it up to the unconscious girls lips but she was only able to dribble a few drops into her mouth.

"Can we move her?" Meldiron asked.

Thia pursed her lips considering. "Not far if we want her to live." She looked up at them. "We'll have to make camp here until she is well enough to travel."

"Then what?" Mina couldn't help asking.

"Then we take her with us," Thia said softly.

Arion turned back to them abruptly. "Why would we do such a thing?" he demanded, rage simmering in his voice.

"Because… " Thia said quietly as she gently lifted the girl revealing her left shoulder. "She, too, is Marked."

CHAPTER FIVE

Teague paced his chamber restlessly. His last dreamwalk with Thia had left him anxious and irritable. Why was she not coming to the Refuge in the Eastern Mountains? It was like they were trying to keep her away from him. And he needed Thia right now. He'd never needed her more. Caedmon was gone - had been gone almost from the moment they arrived. He was on yet another mission to find more Marked children for Bellasiel and Omen to train.

Teague stopped pacing and shook his head in disgust. He'd seen enough of what they were doing with the children to know it was wrong.

Bellasiel tried to tell him that they were helping those children. She reasoned that as Marked Ones they would have to be prepared to defend themselves from enemies for the rest of their lives. But what Teague had seen when he'd stumbled into the common area two days ago made his stomach churn.

Children as young as three years of age were gathered in military formation in the vast cavern, a relict of when this place had been a great silver mine and had been stripped of its precious metals. They lived underground now, out of necessity, with daylight only seen on the rare occasions when a load of supplies was brought to them. That, too, was something Bellasiel insisted was for their own safety but it didn't take a genius to know that children needed to have fresh air and sunshine to thrive.

Teague had been growing more and more suspicious that the plan Bellasiel had laid out for them in Séreméla was only a small part of the story. There was no way they could have prepared this place, an old abandoned mine, in the manner that it had been prepared had they not been working on it for years.

The original mining tunnels and caverns had been reinforced and expanded. Teague looked around the chamber that he had been given. Elder architects were legendary for being able to work with nature to produce some of the most stunning buildings ever created. Here instead of working with trees and water, as was their norm, they'd worked with rock and mountain. Teague was sure they'd played a role in creating this place. There was no other explanation for its design.

Despite it being entirely underground it was magnificent. The detail that had gone into the rooms was stunning. Even by torchlight Teague recognized that.

But the beauty of this place did not shake Teague's unease. He sat down on his bed and put his head in his hands. Why was Thia not coming? She kept making excuses. A black thought entered his mind. Was Thia staying away because that's what Bellasiel and Omen wanted? Was she following orders and purposely staying away from him?

He shook his head immediately, trying to clear such thoughts from his brain. Thia would never do that to him. He could trust her, if no one else.

Caedmon was a different story. His brother seemed to have bought wholeheartedly into this little plan that Bellasiel had cooked up for them. He was only too eager to disappear at regular intervals with Kiara and bring back more of the children they found. They'd brought so many young ones to the Refuge, Teague was beginning to question their methods. Did they merely steal the children? Did they even talk to the parents? Some of the children were extremely distressed when they arrived.

Not that Bellasiel had let Teague see too many of the children after they arrived. She was very careful to keep him far away from their barracks. But Teague could still hear the littlest of them crying for their mothers at night. The mineshafts carried all sorts of noises. That's how Teague had discovered the training area. When he had questioned its existence with Bellasiel and Omen, they had used their fancy talk to move his mind away from his suspicions.

They'd been doing that from the start. Neither of them liked to be questioned and when Teague asked even the most innocent of questions, they would steer the conversation away. Or worse tried to rationalize his worries.

Omen said his suspicions were because of the constant stress he was under from the *Draíodóir*. Omen had once trained with the *Draíodóir*. Teague had been surprised when he met him. He was a gaunt grey man - there was no other way to describe him. He had no hair, grey eyes, and a grey beard. He wore all grey clothing. Even his skin had a faintly grey tinge to it but Teague didn't know if that was from the poor lighting in the mine or the fact that his skin merely reflected his clothing.

Cathi Shaw

It was rare for one to have left the *Draíodóir* training. The *Draíodóir* recruited their members from a young age; Teague himself had started training with them when he was only six. The *Draíodóir* often were the only family their members could recall. One did not just leave them. There were probably only a handful of men who had done so over the last hundred years. And Omen was one of those men.

Teague didn't know how many years Omen had spent training with the *Draíodóir* but it was clear that he'd been at least as advanced (if not as skillful) as Teague when he left. And he seemed to have been able to break all ties with the brotherhood, which should have been encouraging to Teague but only made him more suspicious of the older man. Omen insisted he was trying to help Teague break his own ties from them. A job that was proving excruciatingly difficult and one Teague could only describe as a miserable experience.

The first task Omen wanted to help Teague achieve was to build a rock solid mental block in his mind. Because all *Draíodóir* were linked mentally, Omen rationalized that it would be the only way for Teague's mind to be truly free. Then they could start severing the ties to the *Draíodóir* one by one. Even Omen recognized and admitted the monumental task that lay before them.

Teague had been seen as especially important to the *Draíodóir*, not just because he was a Marked One but also because of his special abilities. He was one of the most talented *Draíodóir* novices to ever have been found - and that had been when he was six. The *Draíodóir* claimed to not know the reasons that Teague was so gifted but after Thia had told him about their time with the People and revealed that Teague and her were actually Halfings, he suspected that it was his genes that made the difference. But Omen didn't know about that. Teague and Thia had kept their origins a secret from everyone except their siblings. Celeste, the leader of the Undergrounders, had insisted on secrecy and Thia felt bound by her promise to the People to keep it. Teague, who had been manipulated for years by the *Draíodóir*, was only too happy to keep her secret. There were few people he trusted and Thia was one of them.

Despite Omen's claims that he wanted to help him, over the last few weeks Teague had become more and more distrustful toward the older man. Sometimes he'd felt manipulated by him. Other times he'd caught Omen watching him with an almost eager gleam in his dull grey eyes. And last week, he'd come across Omen and Bellesiel talking in urgent whispers. He'd not caught what they were saying but there was something about their tone and the way they stopped immediately when he arrived that pricked his suspicions even further.

Despite his distaste for the man, Teague had to admit that Omen's teachings had been somewhat successful. Within days of arriving at the Refuge Teague had been able to easily construct the mental wall that blocked his mind from the other *Draíodóir*. Bellasiel had been especially relieved when Omen and Teague had told her it was done.

For Teague it was odd. For the first time since early childhood, his mind was empty. The *Draíodóir* mind connection had been a part of him for so long that he suddenly felt lonely. It was hard to explain the connection to others. It wasn't as if the *Draíodóir* could read his thoughts or command him to do things; it was more like his connection to Thia when she was close. They could communicate. Omen had insisted it was more than just communication; he claimed the *Draíodóir* were manipulating Teague.

But part of Teague had to question Omen's reasoning. It had been easy to shut off his connection to the others. Almost too easy. If they were able to control him, Teague believed the *Draíodóir* would not make it so easy for a single member to disconnect from them. There was a tickle in the back of his mind that questioned what Omen and Bellasiel wanted him to believe.

Teague stood up and looked at the door of his chamber. He wasn't a prisoner in the mine; he could wander wherever he wanted. But Bellasiel and Omen had encouraged him to spend time in meditation. They suggested it would clear his mind. And Omen always provided the meditation task.

Teague wasn't so sure their motives were innocent. He was beginning to wonder if they encouraged the meditation so that he wouldn't go and see what was going on in the Refuge itself.

Teague narrowed his eyes. There was a small army of Helpers who ran the Refuge. People from all areas of the Five Corners had been found who were willing to help *The Cause*.

Teague snorted. *The Cause*, as Bellasiel liked to call it, was originally to keep the six Chosen Ones safe. But Teague was the only one of the original six who had been here for any length of time. Mina, Meldiron and Thia were hunting for a missing Marked One down South and Caedmon and Kiara had delivered him to the Refuge and then immediately disappeared on their scouting missions.

And this place had been build for more than just the six of them. It was clearly outfitted for hundreds, if not thousands of people. Bellasiel seemed to be on her way to collecting that many of the Marked Ones.

Teague had to wonder why they would bring this many Marked Ones to one place. He didn't think it was just to keep them safe. Last week when he stumbled upon the enormous training room and the children in lines doing military exercises it had suddenly become crystal clear. He now knew - they were building the army of Marked Ones that the Prophecy mentioned.

Teague knew more about the Prophecy than anyone realized. It was as if they had all forgotten that the *Draíodóir* were the ones who had interpreted the Prophecy for the Elders. Teague, while only a novice, was still part of the inner circle of *Draíodóir*. He was privy to what the Prophecy hinted at, even if he hadn't actual been able to read the ancient script himself.

Everyone seemed so focused on what the Prophecy said about the unborn child of the Chosen Marked Ones that they ignored what the other, more important, parts of the scroll said about the Marked Ones as a whole. From what Teague had understood the Prophecy spoke of an uprising of the people, a uniting of forces, led by the Marked Ones. There were also warnings of manipulation and power – not necessarily by the Marked Ones but by those who would control them. The Army that Bellasiel seemed to be intent on building with the children was also mentioned. Except … Teague couldn't remember all of it. When he'd been introduced to the Prophecy it had not been so important to him. He'd not realized that the small circle on his left shoulder was the Mark (although he suspected the *Draíodóir* knew it all along).

What he really needed was to see a copy of the Prophecy in person. He shook his head. But that was looking more and more unrealistic since he was stuck in the Refuge. And the longer he was stuck here the more he had to question Bellasiel and Omen's sincerity in helping him and his friends. Worse of all, he was beginning to question whether he would ever see Thia again.

Finding Refuge

CHAPTER SIX

Travelling with the large number of children meant slow progress. It also meant frequent stops for supplies. Twenty-five children ate a lot - especially when many of them weren't used to having full bellies. Unfortunately that was most of the children given the increasing lack of food in the Five Corners due to the drought. Kiara couldn't wait until they got to the Refuge with them. She wasn't sure how she did it but Bellasiel always ensured that there was plenty of food in the Refuge. It was almost as if she'd been planning and stockpiling it for some time.

With such a large group they were forced to camp on the outskirts of towns and villages to avoid being seen. Caedmon, with his gift for finding shelters in the most improbable of places, continued to surprise Kiara with the campsites he created. They were hidden from the more travelled roads and, more often than not, included natural play areas for the children (a swimming hole or a grove of trees where they could play hide and seek). That had been another surprise from Caedmon. He was amazingly good with children – far better than she was. Watching him with even the smallest of their charges, warmed Kiara's heart in a way that made her uncomfortable.

Still having to find camp outside the towns and villages, meant for an onerous trip. Thankfully they had sympathizers in almost every part of the Five Corners and they were kept well supplied with food and other necessities.

Caedmon and her took turns going into the various towns and hamlets to pick up supplies. Today it was Kiara's turn. Surprisingly the sympathizers she was seeing today were people she knew. She had stayed at this very Inn in Green Lake when they'd travelled through the mountains last winter. The couple was very nice but she'd had no idea at the time that they were helping the Marked Ones.

"Well, here are the supplies you need," the man, Haros, said with a smile.

"Thanks," Kiara said, hoisting the sacks of supplies onto her back and preparing to leave.

"Um, Miss," his wife beckoned to her from the side of the Inn.

Kiara frowned and put the sacks down on the ground. She needed to get back to the camp where Caedmon was trying to keep too many hungry children quiet. They had been running low on supplies for several days now and the kids were becoming more and more irritable. Even though he didn't seem to mind, Kiara didn't want to leave Caedmon to try to keep them happy for too long. But she pasted a smile onto her face and followed the woman to her kitchen.

She led Kiara to a small pantry cupboard and opened the door. Squatting inside on the floor of the tiny room was the filthiest, skinniest child Kiara had ever seen. And she'd seen some pretty dirty ones in her recent travels.

"Her mother sent her to us two days ago asking that we pass her on to you."

Kiara looked at the woman. "She's Marked?"

The woman wrinkled her nose and said dubiously, "That's what her mother says."

Kiara wondered what made the Innkeeper's wife so distrustful. There were Marked Children scattered throughout the Five Corners, more than they'd ever imagined. It wasn't out of the realm of possibilities that one would be found here.

Kiara squatted down so that she was at eye level with the child. The little girl had long, matted dark hair and enormous dark eyes in a painfully thin face. She was looking at her feet shyly.

"What's your name?" Kiara asked softly.

The girl looked up and then looked down again. "Deanna," she whispered. Kiara noticed how she almost folded into herself when she spoke, as if she was terrified of doing something wrong and just wanted to disappear.

Kiara stood up. "Well, I guess I can take her with us."

The woman sniffed. "That's mighty kind of you, Miss Kiara, but just remember you're not running a charity."

Kiara turned and looked at the woman closely. Her mouth was pinched in disapproval.

"What do you mean?"

"If she's Marked, I'll eat Haros' hat. Her mother's a good-for-nothing who's just trying to get rid of one of her mistakes."

Kiara looked back at the child, cowering now in the pantry. "Deanna, come out here please," she said.

The little girl hesitated and then crawled out of the pantry.

"Why did your mother send you here?" Kiara asked.

Deanna bit her lip and rubbed her grubby hand across her dripping nose. "'Cause of the scar," she said timidly.

"The scar?" Kiara repeated.

"Uh-huh. Ma said you was taking all of us kids with the scar and keeping us safe."

"Hmmm," Kiara said, her suspicions pricked. "Can you show me your scar?"

Deanna looked up at her distrustfully.

"We don't take anyone with us unless they can show us they have the scar," Kiara told her when the girl remained silent.

Deanna seemed to think about that for a moment then she nodded. She pulled her filthy dress off her right shoulder to reveal a black smudge.

Kiara reached out and touched Deanna's shoulder. Clearly someone who had never seen the Mark had tried to draw something meant to resemble it onto the girl.

Kiara looked at the innkeeper's wife and shook her head. Why would a parent do this to such a small child? Kiara couldn't believe that a mother would disown a 6-year old. Children could be irritating, yes, but Kiara couldn't imagine someone trying to get rid of their child, especially if she wasn't Marked.

Suddenly Kiara wanted to see for herself this woman who called herself a mother.

"Deanna, can you take me to your mother?" Kiara asked the little girl.

Deanna eyes widened in fear. She shook her head. Kiara frowned. It appeared that the mother was the source of the girl's terror. Kiara felt her temper flare.

She knelt down in front of the little girl and forced herself to speak gently despite the anger bubbling inside, "You're not in trouble, honey, but I do need to speak to your mother."

Deanna bit her lip and seemed to be considering. Then her shoulders slumped in defeat. "Okay," she whispered.

"I'll be back for the supplies," Kiara told the Innkeeper's wife.

She followed the little girl through the village to the outskirts of Green Lake. There, on the edge of town, was a tiny shack that looked in danger of falling over.

"She'll be in here - she sleeps this time of day," the girl told Kiara.

Kiara followed Deanna up to the house, trying to imagine what kind of mother would be sleeping in mid-afternoon. Brijit would never have taken to her bed when the sun was still in the sky! Not while she was well at least.

"Ma?" the little girl yelled. A small boy about a year or two younger than Deanna opened the door.

"Shh, Deanna, she be sleeping. You don't wanna wake her, do you?"

"This lady wants to see her."

The boy looked up at Kiara dubiously then without saying another word ran past her and around the side of the shack.

"He's making himself scarce," Deanna told her solemnly. "Ma ain't gonna be too happy to be woke up."

Kiara wrinkled her forehead. She didn't like the sound of this.

"Ma!" Deanna called again. "Did what you told me but the lady wants to see you."

A few minutes later a tired and nasty looking woman stumbled to the door.

"What are you doing back here?" she snarled at the girl. Deanna didn't even flinch. Clearly she was accustomed to being spoken to this way.

"Lady wants to see you."

Only then did she see Kiara. "Well, you takin' the Marked Ones - so take her. She's Marked."

Kiara could see a smaller girl clinging to her mother's skirts. The woman pushed her back inside, the child fell over and started wailing. Then another child started crying from somewhere in the house.

The woman stepped out and closed the door but the wails could still be heard.

"The problem is that your daughter isn't Marked, is she?" Kiara said testily.

The woman turned to Deanna. "What did you do?" she snarled at her.

"I done what you told me to," the girl protested stepped back and flinching.

"We don't take children who aren't Marked," Kiara said firmly.

"Git inside then." The woman reached out and grabbed Deanna by the hair. The girl howled in pain and the woman quickly backhanded her across the mouth "Shuddup."

"Wait." Kiara stepped forward. "You can't treat her like that."

"I can treat her any way I want," the woman said looking Kiara up and down distastefully. "Nothing a freak like you can do about it."

Kiara drew herself up to her full height, towering over the horrid creature in front of her. She made a split second decision. "Deanna, come along with me," she said to the girl who was sniffling and trying not to cry out in pain. Her dirty cheek was brightly outlined with an imprint of her mother's hand.

"What you doing?" the woman asked.

"I guess I was mistaken. I think Deanna is Marked after all," Kiara said and took the girl gently by the arm. "She'll be safe with us. Something that she won't be here with you."

Kiara was silent on the way back to camp. She couldn't get the hatred that had been apparent in the woman's eyes out of her head. She wondered what would have happened to Deanna if she'd left her with her mother.

Later that night, Caedmon sat beside her watching the fire burn low.

"You can't pick up every mistreated child and orphan, Kiara," he said reasonably as he sharpened his dagger.

Kiara sighed. "I know, Caedmon, I know. But I couldn't just leave her there." She put her head on his shoulder. "What would you have done?"

He was silent, his eyes on the dagger. After a few moments he said, "I don't know."

"Next time you go for supplies," Kiara said softly. "The sooner we get back to the Refuge the better."

#

By the time they arrived at the Refuge, Kiara was hot, tired and irritable. Twenty-six whiney children, many of them starting to miss home, were grating. She was looking forward to cleaning up and having some time to herself.

Kiara sighed. The older children had tried to keep the young ones quiet but by the end of the journey they were all exhausted.

Bellasiel met them in the main chamber of the mine. Her eyebrows rose when she saw the numbers.

"You've been busy," she observed, pleasure infusing her words. "People can't wait to get rid of these ones."

Caedmon explained, "The draught is taking its toll." There had been little rain in most of the Five Corners for the past three months. It had been a hot summer. Crops were suffering and if it continued there was a fear that the next winter would be hard everywhere. If people could get rid of a few hungry mouths to feed, then they would do so.

"There's also been more activity by the Hunters," Caedmon went on. "It's put families on high alert. There are rumors circulating that entire families protecting their Marked child have been slaughtered. People are nervous and more willing to give them up."

He looked around the room silent for a moment. "What's been happening here?" Caedmon finally asked.

"The ones you found earlier have commenced training. Caedmon, now that you are here you can help with that." Bellasiel paused, an eager light in her eyes. "Have you found any older ones yet?"

Kiara shook her head. Bellasiel's eyes reflected her disappointment. The oldest child they had discovered was 13. Kiara knew they all had to be thinking the same thing. Were they the only Marked Ones their age that existed? They knew that the older the Marked Ones were, the more chance there was that they'd mate and reproduce. And the Prophecy spoke of a child born of two Marked Ones who would result in the end of an age. But that was all they knew. At least that was all that Bellasiel admitted to knowing.

What they really needed was a complete copy of the Prophecy. They'd almost had that - Mina had one sitting on her desk the entire time she was in Séreméla but she'd not realized how vital it was. And by the time she did realize the importance of the document, it had been stolen and the great Elder Archivist, Eöl Ar-Feiniel, had been murdered.

That had been a great loss. Even if they found a complete copy of the Prophecy, it would take time to attempt a translation as it was written in an ancient dialect of the Elder language. All they knew of the Prophecy was from small excerpts translated by the *Draíodóir* and everyone knew they weren't trustworthy.

Which brought Kiara's thoughts back to Teague, Caedmon's brother who was a novice *Draíodóir*. Teague was the reason they'd had to come to the Eastern Mountains so quickly in the Spring. Bellasiel had been worried that Teague would be corrupted by the *Draíodóir* before they could safely get away. Even Teague himself had admitted that he'd been overpowered by a group of *Draíodóir* when he'd been dragged before the

Elder council. He was one of the main reasons they'd left Séreméla in such haste.

Of course he wasn't the only reason, Kiara admitted, remembering the death of Brijit, her adopted mother. She pushed the memory away.

"How's Teague?" she asked instead.

Bellasiel looked grim. "Oh that's another thing. I have some news and you're not going to like it."

Finding Refuge

CHAPTER SEVEN

Kiara followed Caedmon through the tunnels towards Teague's chambers. She had to jog to keep pace with him; he was walking so fast.

Caedmon had only listened to Bellasiel for three minutes before he'd stormed out of the room. Bellasiel had explained that Omen and her were becoming increasingly concerned for Teague's wellbeing.

"His link with the *Draíodóir* is strong," she'd noted. "They knew from the start that Teague was special and so they've bound him to them more firmly than I've ever seen. Omen, himself, has never seen such a weaving of the links throughout a novice's brain." Bellasiel had shaken her head. "I fear for his sanity if we keep pushing him and trying to sever the links."

Caedmon had looked grim.

"And I'm beginning to fear that the pressure of the last few months is already starting to threaten his sanity," Bellasiel had added.

That was when Caedmon had left. Kiara knew that he was angry from the way he was holding himself. Caedmon rarely lost his temper but when his anger flared it was dangerous and dark. He clearly didn't believe Bellasiel and she knew that he didn't trust Omen, the former *Draíodóir* apprentice who said he was trying to help Teague. Caedmon had been surly every time Kiara had tried to talk to him about Teague's therapy. He wasn't happy with what was being done to his brother.

"Caedmon, can you slow down a bit?" Kiara called as she followed him deeper into the mine but he ignored her and she knew better than to push him.

Finally he came to a halt in front of Teague's chambers.

Caedmon pounded on the door. "Teague!" he called.

A moment later Teague opened the door. Kiara could only stare at him. His hair was rumpled as if he'd been running his hands through it, the curls even wilder than normal. And his eyes, always strange with the rare silver color, had a wild gleam in them.

"Did they send you?" he asked Caedmon aggressively.

"What are you talking about?" Caedmon asked him, his tone bewildered.

Teague pushed passed Caedmon to stick his head in the hallway and looked frantically up and down as if searching for something. He stopped when he saw Kiara standing in the hallway behind his brother. Then he motioned for them both to come in.

"Are you sure they didn't send you?" he asked again, rubbing his arms and beginning to pace around the room.

"No one sent us," Caedmon answered patiently. "We just returned."

Teague stopped pacing and looked them with an expression of horror. "You didn't bring more of the children here, did you?"

Kiara nodded. "Of course we did, Teague. Those children are going to be killed if we don't bring them to the Refuge."

But Teague was shaking his head and moaning. "No! Don't you see? That's what *they* want."

"That's what who wants, Teague?" Caedmon asked, his brow furrowed in confusion. He exchanged a look with Kiara. Teague was talking nonsense.

"The Enemy. They want them here so they can build an army and kill us all." He began smacking himself on the head. "Can't help them."

"Teague?" Caedmon said sternly but Teague was mumbling to himself in *Draíodóir* tongue.

Kiara looked a Caedmon questioningly. He shook his head.

"Teague. Calm down."

Suddenly Teague stopped and glared at Kiara.

"Where's your sister? Where is Thia? Why doesn't she come? Why?"

Kiara shook her head. "Teague, I don't know where Thia is. We can only contact her through you and your dreamwalks, remember? You know where she is better than I do."

Teague began pacing again. "They are still in Sailsburg. They are keeping her away on purpose. Want her away from me."

"Who wants her away from you?" Kiara asked, trying to understand Teague's manic mumblings.

"I told you, the Enemy," Teague screamed violently, spit flying from his lips in Kiara's direction.

Caedmon turned to her. "Kiara, I think you'd better leave us alone."

"But-" she started to argue.

Caedmon gave her a hard look then he closed his eyes and took a deep breath. He put his hands on her shoulders and pulled her close. "I need to speak to my brother privately," he whispered in her ear. "Please, Kee."

Feeling inexplicably hurt, Kiara nodded. Teague was raving in the corner again. She had no idea what Caedmon planned to do to calm him, but it was clear that he didn't want her to witness it.

#

Kiara was able to wash the dust off and have a real meal before Caedmon came and found her in her chamber. It was obvious that he, on the other hand, hadn't taken the time to clean up from their journey. He looked tired and worried as he splashed water from the basin in the corner onto his grimy face.

"How is Teague now?" she asked, as she put a plate of food on the small table for him.

Caedmon sat and shook his head, his long hair coming loose from the leather tie. Kiara ached to smooth it back for him but he was sending out clear signals that he didn't want to be touched. "I've never seen him like that before. He did calm down a bit after you left but he was still so agitated."

Kiara sat down across from him. "It's obvious that something is seriously wrong with Teague."

Caedmon gave her a black look, his mouth pressed shut.

"It's true - you saw him, Caedmon. I'm not saying it's Teague fault. I'm just worried that the stress of all of this is getting to him." She paused. "What have Bellasiel and Omen done to his mind so far?"

Caedmon picked up a chicken leg and began to systematically shovel food into his mouth. For a moment, Kiara lost track of what she'd been saying as she wondered if Caedmon was even tasting his food. Caedmon, after being in the Army for so many years, had amazing survival skills. He would eat almost anything and could sleep anywhere in order to keep his energy up.

As he continued to shovel food into his mouth, he started talking, "Last time I spoke with him, Omen said that Teague had been able to successfully build a mental block between the *Draíodóir* and his brain. He could keep them out but it was fatiguing. Omen had been worried that the stress of maintaining that block would wear on Teague."

Kiara nodded, remembering the wild look in Teague's eyes. "Do you think that's what's happened?"

Caedmon chewed his food thoughtfully. He seemed to be mulling things over but his expression was grim.

"What are you thinking?" Kiara asked, worry infusing her words.

Caedmon put down the chicken leg and looked at Kiara. His dark eyes were unreadable. "That theory does make sense but ..." he paused.

"But what? No one blames Teague for what the *Draíodóir* have done to his mind. We all know just powerful they are."

Caedmon nodded. "I know that but something Teague said made me examine things more closely."

"What do you mean?"

"Well," Caedmon paused, his brow furrowed. Then he went on reluctantly, "What if he's right, Kiara?"

Kiara stared at Caedmon hardly believing her ears. Had he lost his mind now as well? But Caedmon went on before she could say anything.

"It *is* possible. Think about it. Who told us about the Refuge in the Eastern Mountains? Who brought us here? Who insisted that Teague needed help from Omen?"

Kiara paused. Bellasiel *had* suggested all those things. But Meldiron, the Elder prince and Mina's long lost brother, had insisted that she was trustworthy and it seemed that the Elder healer had just as much to lose as they did if they were caught. What Caedmon was suggesting was crazy. But how well did they know Meldiron even? Come to think of it, how much did they know of the Elders at all? For most of her life, Kiara knew Elders as far off, mystical people who kept to themselves. Could it be that none of them were to be trusted?

"Is Teague saying that Bellasiel and Omen are working for the Enemy?" Kiara asked slowly as she digested Caedmon's words.

He nodded.

"And you believe him?" She whispered, studying his serious face. Kiara looked down. She didn't want to believe this – it complicated things too much. It was easier to just believe Bellasiel's original story. And for once in her life Kiara longed for something that was simple. Life had become entirely too complicated in the last year.

But Kiara remembered the wild look in Teague's eyes. It was as if he was losing his mind. Could they really trust him in his current mental state?

"Caedmon, you saw your brother. Something is seriously wrong with him. He isn't functioning like a sane person," she said hesitantly. Caedmon's face darkened. "I'm not saying Teague is wrong, I'm just saying we should be careful about believing anything he says in the state he's in."

Caedmon pushed his plate away, his remaining food uneaten, and stood up. "What if what he says makes sense, Kiara?"

"It doesn't!" she said, ignoring the fact that her voice was rising. What Caedmon was suggesting couldn't make sense. It would change everything. What would it mean for the children they had brought to the Refuge? What would it mean for any of them if this were true? It was easier to believe that something was wrong with Teague than to imagine the opposite.

"You didn't hear everything he had to say."

Kiara stood up herself and shook her head. "No, I didn't. And I don't want to hear it now. Teague needs help. Aren't you worried about what his erratic behavior could mean for the rest of us?"

Caedmon turned away from her and Kiara felt a prick of guilt. Teague was Caedmon's brother after all. How would she feel if someone were speaking this way about Mina or Thia?

She took a deep breath, striving for a neutral tone. "Caedmon, I know you love Teague but think about this rationally for a minute."

Caedmon turned back to her, his eyes blazing. "Are you calling me irrational, too, now Kiara?"

"No! That's not what I meant," Kiara said desperately, tears filling her eyes. She hated fighting with Caedmon.

"Then what do you mean?" he asked angrily.

"If Teague lets down his mental block with the *Draíodóir*, which he might do if he truly believes Bellasiel and Omen are the enemy, then he will lead all of the ones trying to kills us right to this spot. Why would Bellasiel and Omen collect all the Marked Ones together if they wanted to kill us? They've had plenty of opportunity to kill us but they haven't. Think about it Caedmon, it doesn't make sense."

"Doesn't it? Collecting all of us together and then killing us in one spot makes perfect sense."

Kiara stared at him. His mouth was set in a stubborn line. She couldn't believe that Caedmon was buying Teague's story so thoroughly. Couldn't he see how unstable his brother was? She ignored the little voice in the back of her head that said Caedmon might be right.

"I don't think they mean to kill us," she insisted. She wouldn't believe it. They'd been helping them. They had to be. She refused to consider the alternative. For if Bellasiel and Omen were working against them as Teague believed then what would it mean for the children she'd brought here all summer? Could it be that she wasn't rescuing them at all but leading them to a fate that could be worse than death?

Caedmon shook his head at her. "Maybe they don't mean to kill us but they sure as hell want to build an army, don't they? The children we've brought have already started training and they want me to help." He paused. "I'm telling you Kiara, whether Teague's story is the truth or not, something isn't right here."

Fear caused Kiara's throat to tighten and she shook her head in denial. "I don't believe it," she whispered hoarsely, "I can't."

Caedmon turned away and strode toward the door.

"Where are you going?" she asked softly. They hadn't been alone together in months, not since they first left on the first mission to find the children. She'd been hoping to have some time with Caedmon and not spend it fighting. But his shoulders were still set rigidly, a sure sign that he was still angry.

"I need to think this through," he told her.

"Now?" she asked, hating the neediness that was in her voice but unable to stop it.

Caedmon closed his eyes. She walked over to him and cupped his cheek with her hand. "Can't you stay for a bit?"

But when Caedmon opened his eyes, Kiara saw his mind was made up. His voice came out gently.

"I'm sorry, Kiara, but I need to figure out how to help Teague. I fear that if we wait on this we could lose him forever.

CHAPTER EIGHT

The girl remained unconscious for the rest of the night but Thia insisted that they take turns sitting with her. Mina noticed that Meldiron volunteered to stay up with her before Arion could do so. She wondered if her brother didn't trust his kinsman to let the girl live? She knew she had her doubts as to whether Arion would harm her. She couldn't explain the rage she'd seen in his face when they'd insisted on sparing the girl's life. It had given her the chills!

Thia had attempted to dreamwalk with Teague that night so she could send a message to the Refuge about their delay but Mina saw that her sister was despondent the next morning. Thia had either been unsuccessful at contacting Teague or she had been disheartened as to what she'd discovered in the dreamwalk with him. Mina didn't want to upset her sister further by asking her directly about it.

Although Mina knew Thia was desperate to get to the Refuge and see for herself what was ailing Teague, she still refused to move her new patient until she was well. Arion started to argue with the decision but surprisingly Meldiron overruled him and Arion would not argue with his crown prince.

Mina saw that the girl's burns were substantial. Thia was gentle with her ointments and salves but the Hunter girl still cried out in pain. Mina tried to help but whenever she went near her the girl became absolutely frantic. Mina told herself to ignore the stab of hurt she felt when the Nasseet girl would howl and hiss at her. She spoke in soothing tones but it was to no avail. Finally Thia, worried that the girl would dislodge her bandages and further damage herself, shooed Mina away.

Mina couldn't say why the girl was so frightened by her. At first she assumed that it was because she was an Elder but she let Meldiron near her and he looked more like an Elder than any of them! Her brother and Thia were the only ones the girl would allow herself fall asleep near. Finally Thia suggested that Mina and Arion keep the camp well stocked and leave the nursing up to her and Meldiron.

Mina couldn't chase the hurt away at first. It appeared that her brother, the Crown Prince of the Elders, was a better nurse than she was. She'd lived with Brijit all her life and her mother had been one of the most gifted healers in the Lowlands. Although Mina hadn't inherited her skill as a healer, she certainly knew how to watch over invalids, having done it enough times at the Inn. But this newcomer was clearly wary of her. Mina couldn't remember anyone ever being afraid of her in her life; it was a new sensation, one she didn't like at all.

"You'll get used to it," Arion told her as they sat across from one another at the fire one night.

"What?" Mina asked, pulled from her thoughts.

"People not trusting you, people judging you, even people hating you, for no reason." Bitterness made his voice rough.

"How did you know what I was thinking?" Mina asked.

"You have a very expressive face, princess. You might wish to learn how to school it before it gives more important things away." Arion stared into the fire moodily.

Mina thought about her face. She'd never known it to be especially expressive but then she'd never given it much thought. And she'd certainly never had anything important to hide from anyone. Did she have something to hide now?

Of course she did. If strangers learned that she and the others were Marked it could cost them their lives. How easy it was to forget.

Mina studied Arion. In the flickering firelight, his features were especially attractive. And the dark hair and brows on an Elder face were a refreshing change. She couldn't seem to pull her gaze away from him. When he suddenly looked up at her, she felt her cheeks heat.

He raised his eyebrows questioningly but Mina looked down, flustered. She was surprised when he broke the uneasy silence with an invitation.

"Tomorrow I'm going early to the shore to see if I can find some clams and crabs. Since we are going to be here for a while, we might as well take advantage of the food supply." He paused and then asked almost reluctantly, "Do you want to come?"

Mina found herself nodding before she'd even processed what he said. She'd never spent time by the sea and she was eager to see what new things she would discover.

"Thank you, I'd like that very much," she said eagerly.

Arion looked at her steadily. "Then you'd better get some sleep. We'll have to be up early." And with that terse announcement he rose and disappeared into the darkness.

Mina sat by the fire a few minutes longer, staring after Arion's large form. Did he want her to come with him in the morning or didn't he? It was hard to tell with the large dark Elder just exactly what he wanted. Shrugging Mina stood up and stretched. Whether he wanted her company or not, she decided to go to bed. She wasn't going to miss an opportunity to discover some of the secrets of the sea!

#

Even though Mina planned to be up early, Arion woke her when it was still dark.

"Princess Minathrial, I am leaving now. Do you still wish to come?"

Mina sat up in a hurry, rubbing the sleep from her eyes. What did he mean did she still wish to come? She wasn't going to miss a chance to learn more about that beautiful sea she'd been catching glimpses of for the last month.

Even though they'd stayed in Sailsburg, a coastal city, Meldiron had not allowed her to wander down to the docks alone. And there didn't seem to be a beach that was close to the city centre where they were staying. Mina had seen the water from her window each day, she'd breathed in the fresh, salty sea air but she hadn't spent time near it. To actually dig in the sand and pull creatures out of the salty water sounded exotic and exciting.

Mina hurried to join Arion on the outskirts of the camp. He was waiting silently in the shadows beneath the trees. He gave her the briefest of nods as she approached. Then they didn't speak but walked through the dunes to the solid sand of the beach.

As they got closer to the shore the distant booming of the waves transformed into a deafening thunder. A thrill of exhilaration shot through Mina. The tide was out but she could just make out the white line of the water as it lapped at the sand in the predawn light. Her hair lifted in the breeze and she laughed spontaneously.

She saw Arion look sideways at her in surprise. Then he shook his head and began to remove his boots.

Mina dropped down onto the sand and began to tug her boots off as well.

"It's so beautiful," she sighed, digging her toes into the smooth sand.

He turned his head to study the ocean in front of him. An expression of confusion flashed across his features. He scrutinized the vast water for a few moments longer then looked down at the bag he'd dropped on the sand.

"It is the sea," he acknowledged flatly as he pulled out a long handled spade from the leather bag at his feet.

"Yes, isn't it amazing?" Mina breathed dreamily.

He was scanning the sand for something and didn't answer. Mina shrugged. Although she didn't know much about him yet, Arion didn't strike her as the type to enjoy the wonders of the world around him. She felt a momentary stab of pity for him and all he was missing.

She began to walk towards that white line that marked where the water met the shore, leaving Arion behind. As she got closer the sea sprayed coolly her in the face and joy rolled through her as the power of the ocean became obvious. Mina closed her eyes and took a deep breath of the salt tainted air, happiness coursing through her.

"Hello," she whispered to the sea and then started walking into it. The water gently lapping at her bare toes was surprisingly warm despite the coolness of the ocean mist. A giggle escaped her lips as she began to wade into the salty depths, drawn by the pull of the magical water.

Suddenly she felt a rough hand on her shoulder pulling her back. Mina opened her eyes, the ocean's magical spell shattered. She was up to her thighs in the water. Arion turned her around.

"What?" she asked irritably.

"Out," he said grimly, as he pulled her back to the shore.

"I was just enjoying the moment," Mina protested.

"By wading to your death?" he asked angrily, his expression dark.

Mina stared at him in surprise. He really *was* angry with her. She didn't understand. All she'd done was greet the sea.

"Tell me this, Princess Minathrial, can you even swim?"

Mina pressed her lips together. Okay so she'd never had the chance to learn how to swim. "I wasn't going to go in that far."

He looked at her hard. "Are you sure? You didn't seem inclined to stop."

Mina was silent.

"We collect the clams over here," he threw over his shoulder as he walked back to where his tools had been left. Mina watched him, her joy shattered.

He looked back at her. "Come on, Princess," he called firmly.

Sighing Mina followed him. "Why don't you call me Mina? Princess is a bit much, don't you think?"

Arion didn't answer her. Instead he picked up his shovel and dug deep into the sand. Then he reached into the hole and began pulling out the shellfish.

Mina exclaimed in delight and quickly picked up the shells he tossed at her feet.

"Put them in the sack," he instructed gruffly and continued to dig the clams out of the wet sand.

After he'd dug up a small pile of the clams he stopped and turned to the East. The sun was just beginning to peak over the horizon and the sky was a beautiful shade of pink. Mina watched in surprise as Arion's features softened and he gazed at the sky with a look of such wistfulness that something in her chest twisted. He truly was beautiful with the morning sun on his face. For once he looked young and carefree.

"Do you know what your name means, Minathrial?" he asked suddenly, his eyes still on the sky.

She shook her head, suddenly eager for the information. "It has a meaning?"

Arion smiled sadly. "In the Elder language it means hope." He turned to her then and Mina's breath caught. His body was silhouetted against the horizon, his eyes hidden in shadow. "You are the princess of hope to our people. And you would throw the meaning of your name away carelessly." Disappointment echoed through his words.

Mina felt a stab of guilt roll over her. It was followed quickly by a spurt of anger that surprised her. "I didn't know the meaning of my name," Mina pointed out, frustration running through her. "You can stop being so high and mighty, Arion. How do you expect me to know my heritage when I wasn't raised as an Elder? It might be what I am physically but mentally I'm a girl from the Lowlands. I have been called Mina all my life. The words *Princess* or *Minathrial* are foreign to me. When someone calls me by those names, I don't feel as if they are talking to the real me." She waved her hand in front of her searching for the right words. "It feels artificial. I don't know what you expect me to be."

He set his mouth grimly then turned and began to gather up his tools. She noticed that he left great pauses in conversations. Mina found the silence jarring. She pushed down her impatience and forced herself to wait for his reply. It wasn't until they were heading back to the camp that it finally came.

"I expect you to be our princess. But you're right I do forget that you are the Lost One. I suppose we all expected you would be returned to us knowing our ways." He stopped and looked at her. "Will you forgive me for being unreasonable with you?"

Mina was surprised. She hadn't taken Arion for one who would apologize lightly. "Of course I will. Will you call me Mina? All my friends do."

Arion shook his head. "I am not your friend. You are my princess and I will only call you Minathrial."

Mina felt a pang of hurt at his words. What did he mean he wasn't her friend? It sounded like he wasn't even willing to consider that they might one day become friends. As though their fate were already decided.

"From the time you were a small girl, I have sworn to protect you," Arion explained as if he had heard her unspoken thoughts and his words explained everything. "But if it makes you more comfortable, I will refrain from calling you princess."

Mina shrugged. "Well, it's better than nothing," she agreed. "Deal." She held out her hand.

Arion looked at her hand with a puzzled expression. "You shake it," she explained. "Like you're agreeing to something. It is a Lowland tradition."

He looked at her dubiously. "You, Minathrial, are nothing as I imagined," he said wryly. For a moment Mina couldn't help wondering what he had expected her to be but before she could ponder that thought for more than a few seconds, he was tentatively taking her hand in his. Mina pumped his hand, enjoying how his strong fingers closed around her own. He held her hand for a moment longer after they finished shaking, then abruptly pulled away.

Mina followed him giving up for the moment on trying to figure out the mystery that was Arion.

CHAPTER NINE

Thia winced as she pulled a dressing from the Hunter-girl's skin. Parts of the girl's thin skin stuck to the linen, causing blood to ooze to the surface. But most of her injuries were healing. Thia could feel the girl watching her with those strange red eyes as she went about her work. The girl never made any sound except when the pain got too much and then small whimpers, the kind an injured animal would make, slipped from her lips.

In fact the girl was silent most of the time except when Arion or Mina came near her. Whenever either of them came within the vicinity, she became agitated and would hiss and mutter in her own language until Thia feared that she'd do harm to herself. It was obvious why the girl feared Arion as he still made it clear that he thought they should let her die. But Thia couldn't fathom why she was so stressed by Mina. And poor Mina was heartbroken. She just wanted to help but she'd come to the conclusion that her presence was only making matters worse so she stayed away. And Thia noticed her sister was spending more and more time with Arion.

Thia wasn't sure how she felt about Mina's attention to the tall, dark Elder. Arion was reserved to the extreme and one could easily see him as cold and uncaring but Thia had seen how his pale eyes followed her sister and softened slightly when Mina exclaimed over a new discovery. Obviously her sister was already special to the Elder. And because of that Thia thought he might be not as unfeeling as he appeared.

On the other hand, it was clear that he didn't approve of the Nasseet girl. He still spoke of leaving her behind on a regular basis. Thia knew he didn't like Hunters but his hatred seemed extreme. And she wondered if it had something to do with Mina? She couldn't say why that thought entered her mind but once it did she couldn't shake it.

Despite the fact that Thia still wanted nothing more than to get back to Teague, she knew that they wouldn't be able to move the girl for at least a week. Teague would just have to hold on for a little bit longer. Thia couldn't risk the girl's life. She just hoped she wasn't putting Teague's life in jeopardy by delaying.

Surprisingly, it was Meldiron who seemed to have a calming influence on the Hunter girl and so he often sat with her allowing Thia to take breaks from her nursing.

It was on the third day after they'd found her that the girl first spoke. Thia and Meldiron had just decided that she mustn't speak their language when she surprised them by speaking aloud.

"Thank you," she said softly, her words heavily accented with the hissing quality that Teague had described the Hunters as having.

Thia had hurried to her side. "You can understand us?" she asked, frantically trying to remember if they had said anything offensive near her. She remembered Arion's latest tirade about leaving her to die and felt a pang of remorse.

She nodded painfully. "Yes. I speak your language."

"What is your name?" Meldiron asked.

"Xyrisse."

Thia held a cup of water up to the girl's lips. She drank thirstily.

"Thank you," she said again after she'd drained the cup.

"We are trying to decide the best way to get you back to your people," Meldiron told her. "We thought if we took you back to Sailsburg we might be able to find a merchant vessel from your homeland."

Xyrisse looked horrified. "You can't send me back to Nasseet," she said, her voice panicked.

Thia reached out and touch her shoulder gently. "If you don't want to go back, we won't make you," she said soothingly hoping to calm her down.

Xyrisse closed her eyes in relief.

Meldiron spoke. "We thought you'd want to go home," he explained.

Xyrisse opened her strange red eyes and looked at him. "You can't send me back," she insisted. "They are the ones who left me for dead."

#

Over the next few days, Xyrisse told her story to Thia and Meldiron. She was too weak to talk for any length of time but finally they began to understand why she did not want to return to her homeland.

Xyrisse had been raised in a family with a high status in Nasseet. She was one of only a few children ever born in that country with the

Mark. But despite the Mark being clearly visible on her translucent skin, she was not discriminated against nor was her life ever in danger due to it.

Xyrisse explained that on Nasseet the highest status was to train as a Hunter. Only a handful of individuals were born with the skills needed to be a Hunter.

"What are those skills?" Meldiron had asked.

Xyrisse smiled grimly. "The ability to teleport, of course. The ability to sense an enemy over far distances. And the ability to kill by feeding."

"Feeding?" Thia asked weakly, feeling mildly sick to her stomach.

"Essentially absorbing the enemy's life force," Xyrisse explained.

Thia remembered how Mina had almost died at the hands of a Hunter and suppressed the urge to shudder in revulsion.

From birth, Xyrisse had been identified as one of the Hunter candidates of her generation. There were six other children born in the same decade as her who were likewise identified. Hunter training began at an early age and typically Hunters were proficient at their skills by their late teens.

Although Xyrisse had trained as a Hunter, she had started to have misgivings about the life expected of her at age 15.

"Why?" Meldiron queried.

She shook her head. "Part of our training required that we teleport with an active Hunter and join him or her on the kill. Too many of those kills were of innocent children." She looked at them with her red eyes. "Based on your friend's reaction to me, I assume you are aware that my people have been loaning out our Hunters as assassins for your extermination of the Marked Ones."

Thia and Meldiron both nodded.

"I did not think it was right to kill children. Even for the prices that were being paid. The Hunters I trained with did not agree with me." She paused. "When I told my father that I would not, *could not*, train with them anymore, he was livid. And the League of Hunters themselves became … aggressive with me."

Thia looked at her. "How so?"

Xyrisse smiled sadly. "I had a little brother," she said softly, her crimson eyes pooling with tears. "They threatened his death unless I agreed to continue my training." She trailed off, falling silent as pink tinged tears dripped down her cheeks.

"What happened?" Meldiron asked gently.

"They killed him. In front of me and with my father's approval."

Thia gasped. She couldn't imagine a parent allowing such a thing.

"When it became clear that I would not, even under the most extreme threats, agree to train, they decided to dispose of me."

"But why didn't they just kill you?" Meldiron asked.

Xyrisse looked at him steadily. "You don't understand. They wanted me to suffer for my insolence. They sentenced me to what is the most painful death to my people: the sun. They brought me over the sea and dumped me in the dunes two days before you came upon me."

"But you can teleport, why did you stay in the sun?"

Xyrisse laughed bitterly. "They made sure I would not be able to escape before they left me."

Thia and Meldiron exchanged a look, neither of them understanding.

"They drugged me with Thistelhorn – a plant that grows on Nasseet and is known to inhibit teleporting."

Thia took her hand. "I'm so sorry."

Xyrisse sighed. "It is not your fault."

Meldiron looked concerned. "What about your Mark? Did they never consider killing you because of it? After all they were hired to kill Marked children."

Xyrisse shook her head. "They were only consigned to kill Marked children in the Five Corners. The people of Nasseet don't consider the Mark a threat."

Thia spoke up. "Can I ask why you are afraid of Arion and Mina?"

Xyrisse laughed bitterly again. "The one you call Arion would kill me if he could. Is it any wonder I don't want him near me?"

Thia nodded in understanding. "But why Mina? She's my sister and I'm sure she is no threat to you."

Xyrisse's eyes narrowed. "You've misinterpreted my reaction to your sister." She paused and seemed to be searching for words. "She attracts me," she finally said.

Meldiron looked shocked.

"What do you mean?" Thia asked carefully.

"It is hard to explain. Let me ask you this: has she ever had contact with a Hunter?" Xyrisse asked

"Yes," Thia admitted. "She was attacked last year."

Xyrisse looked surprised. "How did she survive?"

Thia exchanged a look with Meldiron. She didn't know how she felt about divulging information about Teague.

"The attack was interrupted by a *Draiodóir*," Thia finally said. She didn't need to name Teague specifically.

Xyrisse nodded. "That might explain it. It's faint, the attraction to her is fading but any Hunter in the vicinity would be able to sense her. It's hard to put into words, the feeling. There is an overwhelming urge to drain her of her life spirit, to feast on it."

Thia looked at Xyrisse, horrified.

"I would not choose to do that," Xyrisse assured her. "But it is uncontrollable for a Hunter once the process has been started. She is recovering?"

Meldiron nodded. "She is much better than she was when she first came to Séreméla."

Xyrisse went on. "In time it will fade completely but for now she is in extreme danger from Hunters and you must keep her away from me. I would advise against letting her travel alone in this area. Hunters often come to this shore."

"But we've been on the coast for more than a month now, in Sailsburg," Meldiron pointed out. "We didn't even see a Hunter in the whole time we were there."

Xyrisse nodded. "That makes sense." When Thia and Meldiron exchanged a puzzled look, Xyrisse elaborated, "In a large city it is almost impossible for the Hunters to find a Marked One. That's why the killings always occur in isolated areas. People think it's so there will be no witnesses." Xyrisse paused and laughed hoarsely. "Hunters do not care about witnesses. The only reason for not attacking in a large urban center is that it is too difficult to pinpoint a Marked One. Their energy blends with everyone else's."

Meldiron looked at Thia, his expression grim. "I will tell Arion," he said. "I don't think we should tell Minathrial why she needs an escort at all times. We don't want to frighten her any more than necessary."

Thia nodded in agreement.

"Arion will take his duty to the princess seriously." He paused looking troubled. "Too seriously in some cases. I also would suggest that we not tell him about Xyrisse's attraction to Minathrial."

Thia didn't need convincing. She'd seen Arion's hatred of Xyrisse first hand. She could just imagine how much worse it would be if he knew what she'd just told them.

"We will need to take you with us though, Xyrisse," Thia told her. "You'll have to travel with Mina."

"I'll keep Xyrisse with me on the journey," Meldiron said.

Xyrisse nodded. "That should help. As I mentioned the worse is fading with her and sometimes it dissipates quickly. Sometimes it takes more time."

"When do you think we'll be able to start on the journey again?" Meldiron asked Thia.

Thia looked at Xyrisse. "Her burns on her legs are still quite bad. If she has to ride, I would say another week."

Meldiron nodded. "Here's another thought then. Do you think we should send Minathrial and Arion on ahead of us? If Hunters frequent this shore as much as Xyrisse suggests, then Mina is in grave danger while she is here."

Thia frowned. She was frustrated beyond belief at having to linger so far from Teague but what Meldiron said about Mina made sense.

"Yes," she agreed, "Sending her ahead with Arion is probably the wisest course of action."

"I'll tell them now," Meldiron said.

CHAPTER TEN

Mina stared at her brother in utter shock. Meldiron had just finished telling them that he wanted her and Arion to start the rest of the journey to the Refuge without him and Thia. The plan was that they would follow when Xyrisse had regained enough strength to travel.

"Meldiron, that's ridiculous. Thia is desperate to get to the Eastern Mountains and Teague. There's no reason for us to go on ahead of you. We can wait here and then all travel together."

"I think it is a good idea for us to go ahead," Arion spoke up, surprising Mina even more.

She narrowed her eyes at him. That was the last thing she expected Arion to say. He was still distrustful of Xyrisse and he'd been reluctant to let his Prince, Meldiron, out of his sight in the last few days. He seemed to see himself as Meldiron's personal protector. And she'd noticed that in recent days he seemed to have adopted a similar role with herself. The fact that he was agreeing that they should go ahead was suspicious.

"What does Thia think about this?" Mina asked knowing her sister would see reason.

"She's agreed it would be for the best. Then at least some of our group can arrive in time to assure them that we are all safe and well," Meldiron said.

Mina frowned. There was no way Thia would agree to this so readily. There had to be something they weren't telling her. It had been months since they'd seen the others but Meldiron had never worried about setting their minds at ease before. Why the sudden rush?

Both Elders were closed lipped when she tried to question them further on the topic. Arion just set about preparing their things for travel. Exacerbated, Mina went in search of Thia to find some answers.

But when she spoke to her sister, it was clear that she was in agreement that the best course of action was for Mina and Arion to go on ahead of them.

"Thia, why do you want me to go now? I know you are desperate to get to Teague. It doesn't make sense that we should go ahead."

Thia took a deep breath and then turned to face her. Mina gasped when she saw the look of raw pain on her sister's face. Thia put her hands on Mina's upper arms.

"Please don't question this, Mina. Just go. I can't bear all of us being delayed any longer. At least one of us should get to the Refuge quickly."

Mina looked at her sister closely. Worry creased Thia's face making her look older than her sixteen years. "Is Teague worse?" she asked softly.

Thia's eyes filled with despair. "I don't know," she admitted. "I haven't been able to contact him since we left Sailsburg."

Mina saw the misery on her sister's face and her heart pinched. Poor Thia had been trying to get them to turn Eastward for weeks and now that they were finally doing so, she was stuck; bound by her duty as healer.

"Being stuck here unable to leave …" Thia trailed off as emotion choked her voice. She cleared her throat. "Mina, I need you to go ahead. I can't move Xyrisse and risk her life but I need to know someone is getting closer to Teague and helping him." Tears rolled down Thia's face. "Please don't argue with me about this."

Mina felt a stab of guilt for pushing her sister in such difficult circumstances. She could tell Thia was just barely holding on.

"I'm sorry," Mina said, hugging her sister. "I'll go. Of course I will."

"Thank you." Thia sniffed and wiped her eyes. "Alright let's get you ready to go. I'll braid your hair. Sit down."

Mina sat and felt Thia's hands expertly plaiting her hair. She closed her eyes, relaxing as the familiar sensations washed over her. She could almost imagine they were home in the Inn with Thia doing her hair. So much had happened in the last year. Mina sighed. She loved travelling but there were those times when she missed home. She knew that Thia must miss it more than the rest of them. Her little sister was a true homebody. As Thia tied off the long golden plait, Mina made up her mind. She would do this one thing for Thia without complaint. She would leave her.

#

As Mina put the last few things into her saddlebag, Meldiron approached her.

He smiled. "Be careful, little sister."

Mina raised her brows. "I should be telling you that! You're the one staying here with an injured Hunter. I think you and Thia are probably in more danger than I am." She shook her head at him. Really, everyone was so concerned for her wellbeing but if they stopped to look at it reasonably, she was sure they would see that their fear was misplaced.

Still Meldiron looked unconvinced. "Arion will guard you with his life."

Mina tied down the flap on her saddlebag and turned to face Meldiron. "He shouldn't have to, Meldiron." Her suspicion that something more was behind her brother sending her away returned. "Should he?" She watched the Elder prince closely, wishing she knew his face as well as sister should.

Meldiron looked at her steadily, his green eyes clear. "If he needs to he will."

"Princess Minathrial, are you ready?" Arion's voice rang out from where he was readying his horse. Mina cringed.

"I swear if he doesn't drop the "princess" business, he'll be the one who needs protecting," she told her brother irritably as she swung into the saddle.

Meldiron smiled. "To Arion the proper order of things is very important. You *are* an Elder princess, Minathrial. He just believes that your title should be used."

"Well, I told him to stop it," she answered grumpily, glaring in Arion's direction.

Suddenly she felt Meldiron's hand on her knee. She looked down at her brother surprised by the concern on his handsome face. "Be careful, little sister," he repeated earnestly.

She narrowed her eyes at him. "Why does everyone keep saying that?" she asked.

Meldiron didn't answer for a moment. Then he stepped back and smiled at her. "The Elders have always said that I was the last hope of the Elder people, Minathrial. But they'd forgotten about you. Trust Arion. We will meet again in the Eastern Mountains."

Mina bit her lip, suddenly unsettled by Meldiron's words. She turned her horse to where Arion waited and nodded at him. Then with a final wave to Meldiron and Thia, she cantered out of the dunes behind Arion. For once her excitement at starting a new journey was missing.

#

The first day on the road, passed quickly. While Arion didn't talk to her unless he had to, Mina was happy to take in the sights and sounds around her. They only continued along the coast for the first few hours and then the road turned inward and started to wind in a Northeastern direction through a forest of broad-leafed trees.

They passed no other travelers on the road but there was plenty of wild life in the forest. Exotic birds sang and small strange animals crossed the road at regular intervals, making Mina believe that this was a road less travelled. The woods grew close to the road and it felt as if they were merely riding through the forest itself.

As the sun disappeared behind the trees, Arion led them to a small sheltered clearing in the forest. He dismounted gracefully and began to untie his saddlebags. When Mina remained mounted he looked up at her.

"We will make camp here tonight," he told her.

She nodded and dismounted from her horse, patting her silky mane and murmuring to the gentle animal. The mare that Meldiron had purchased for her was a rich chestnut color with black stockings and kind eyes. She was a beautiful creature and Mina was sure her brother had paid an enormous sum of money for her. But he was the Crown Prince of the Elders and even in exile he had access to resources that she wasn't accustomed to.

"Stella. I think you are a Stella," she told the gentle animal confidently. The horse blinked her enormous liquid brown eyes back at her. Mina had been trying to come up with an appropriate name for her mount since Meldiron had gifted the horse to her. And still she was stumped. Stella was the tenth name she'd tried out.

"You might find more satisfaction if you used an Elder name." Arion's voice behind her made her jump. She hasn't realized he was standing so close.

"An Elder name?" Mina asked, trying to cover her sudden fluster.

"She is an Elder horse."

Mina looked at him sharply. "She is? How do you know?"

Arion shook his head in disappointment. "How could you not?"

Pain filled Mina's chest. Why did he keep punishing her for not knowing the Elder ways. Tears pricked at her eyes as he strode across the clearing and began to set up camp. Mina kept herself busy unsaddling her mare, rubbing her down and tethering her near Arion's mount in knee-deep grass. By the time she was finished the chores she'd calmed down.

She turned to see Arion watching her closely.

"What?" she asked.

"I'm not used to seeing a princess care for her own horse," he answered in a disapproving tone.

Mina felt a prick of anger. "I'm not some helpless girl, you know," she said testily. "Besides who is going to care for my mount here."

He glared at her as if the question was ludicrous.

"You? Come on, Arion, you have enough to do with caring for your own horse and setting up camp." Mina paused at looked back at her mare. "Besides I like caring for her. It makes us closer, which is important if one plans to travel far with her horse. It's important to become friends."

Arion looked at her as though she'd lost her mind.

"What?" Mina asked puzzled.

"A relationship with your mount? The horse is merely the vehicle to get you to where you're going."

Mina stared at him in shock. She was appalled. A horse was so much more than just a means of travel. A horse was a living, breathing creature, a beautiful soul. But she decided not to get into this discussion with Arion. She sensed they would have far different views on the topic.

"I'll go gather some food for us," she said as she walked over to where they'd dumped their saddlebags. She was digging through her bag looking for a bowl she'd packed that would serve well for collecting berries, herbs and tubers when Arion spoke again.

"You will stay here."

Mina stood up and turned around, stunned by the tone of his voice. It was clear that he expected her to obey his orders. But instead of engaging in an argument, Mina decided to take a conciliatory approach.

"Arion, that's ridiculous. We need food to eat. What am I supposed to do in camp, just sit here and watch you build a fire?" She smiled at him.

But he did not smile in return. His lips were set in a tense line and his pale green eyes were even colder than normal.

"You will do as I tell you."

Her attempts at keeping the peace were instantly forgotten. Mina couldn't believe what she was hearing. "Pardon me?" she asked angrily. "Why would I do as you tell me? Am I not your princess? Shouldn't you be doing what I tell you?"

Arion didn't answer.

But Mina's anger flared even hotter. "Or is there something you're not telling me? Are you a prince or a king? Is there some reason you might have that justifies you bossing me around?"

Unconsciously she'd walked across the clearing until she stood directly in front of him, breathing hard with emotion.

Arion looked at a point somewhere behind her left shoulder, still refusing to talk.

"What you have nothing to say? Fine." Mina turned back and grabbed the wooden bowl she'd dropped on the ground. "I'll be back when I've collected some food for the evening meal." She'd only gone halfway across the clearing when Arion's words stopped her cold.

"Your life is in danger and Prince Meldiron asked that you not be let out of my sight."

A shiver ran down Mina's spine. She turned around and searched Arion's face but it was clear that he was serious.

"Who threatens me?" she asked.

He met her eyes. "Hunters," he answered tonelessly.

A stab of terror froze Mina. She forgot to breath, suddenly remembering a dark shadow holding her in its grasp.

"Princess Minathrial?" Arion crossed the clearing until he was an arm's length away. "Are you alright, you've gone very pale."

Mina looked at Arion barely seeing him as the memories came back in abundance. Without another word he took her arm and led her back to the fire pit he'd started to build. He sat her down and then went back to work building the fire. Mina was grateful for the space in which to digest the memories that were flooding back.

The attack in the forest. For months she'd tried to remember it but she'd had no luck. Now, with Arion telling her that she was once more in danger, the memories came tumbling back and were overwhelming in their brutality.

She remembered the red eyes of the creature as it held her in its grasp. Her body had gone numb and then he'd violated her in ways unimaginable.

"It felt as though everything that defined me was being exposed and devoured," she whispered hoarsely as the memories flooded back. "As if all that would be left at the end was darkness and despair." She began to shiver with the memory.

She was vaguely aware of Arion moving to her side but the memories assaulted her and she was in a different clearing in a different forest.

Suddenly she felt Arion's arms around her. "Princess Minathrial. You are safe. Let it go," he was saying softly. "Holding on to these kinds of memories will destroy you."

Mina looked up at him suddenly aware that the clearing was dark. How long has she been sitting like this, stuck in her memories? How long had Arion been holding her?

"You are safe." She could feel his words vibrating through his chest into her back.

Mina nodded, suddenly uncomfortable.

"I'm okay now," she whispered needing there to be space between the two of them.

Arion let go of her and stood. Mina felt the coolness of the night close in around her but it wasn't the same as the icy coldness of her memories. Arion turned back to the fire he had prepared and lit it.

"What makes you think it's me the Hunters are looking for?" she asked finally, not sure she really wanted to hear the answer.

Arion put a small bowl of nuts and dried fruit in her lap before he sat down opposite from her and began to eat.

"It was Xyrisse, actually. I suppose saving her had some use."

Mina was puzzled. Arion seemed to read her emotion.

"You recall how she reacted whenever you tried to go near her?"

"Yes, she was very frightened of me. I still don't understand why," Mina murmured remembering the violent reactions the Hunter girl had shown whenever Mina came near.

Arion shook his head. "That's what we thought - that she was frightened. But she told Thia and Meldiron that it was because you drove her into frenzy. As a Hunter she had an uncontrollable desire to finish what had been started last year. To drain you."

Mina looked at Arion in horror. "She said that. Are you certain?"

He nodded. "She didn't think you'd be safe around her. She was the one who urged us to start on the road. But she also told us that you were in terrible danger along the coast. If she was so attracted to you even when close to death, then other healthy Hunters would also be drawn to you. You are like a beacon flashing in a dark night to them."

Mina swallowed. But then she thought of something. "Why wasn't I attacked in Sailsburg then? I thought that was a main trading centre for the Hunters."

Arion nodded. "It is but with so many people in the city you would be almost impossible to pinpoint. That's why most of the killings of the Marked Ones we've found have been in outlying areas. Almost no dead ones have been found in the cities. The Hunters' tracking abilities are muted in populated areas."

"Will I always be a draw for Hunters?" She asked horrified at the thought.

Arion shook his head. "Xyrisse indicated that even now it was fading but that it would take time for the marker from your attack to completely disappear. She didn't know how long it would take for that to happen but she did say that until that was gone you would be in terrible danger."

"So we started to the Eastern Mountains to put distance between us and the Hunters?"

Arion nodded. "And you understand now why you must not wander off by yourself?" he asked sternly.

Mina shivered as she remembered the cold embrace of the Hunter who'd almost killed he, then she nodded in agreement. She never wanted to experience such a thing again.

"We will travel quickly, Princess. The greater distance we put between ourselves and Nasseet the better."

CHAPTER ELEVEN

The first two days of travel were uneventful. Now that Mina knew why they had been so adamant that she leave camp, she focused on putting as much distance between herself and the coast. Arion woke her in the early hours of the morning, before the sun brightened the Eastern sky, and they rode hard into the late evening.

Mina wondered if Arion ever slept. He was always awake and sitting up, his light eyes scanning the forest as she fell asleep each night and it was he who woke her each morning. She could barely keep her eyes open after they had their meager meal each night. She wondered how the Elder did it.

They didn't speak much on the ride - they were pushing their horses hard and the focus was on escape rather than conversation. But despite the stressful situation, Mina felt oddly at peace with Arion. The afternoon in the clearing, when he sat with her through the horrible memories seemed to have cemented their relationship. It was as if they didn't need to speak to feel comfortable with one another.

In the late afternoon of their third day, Arion led them to a clearing for camp much earlier than the other days.

"The horses are fatiguing," he told her grimly as they dismounted and unsaddled their mounts.

Mina nodded. Her strong mare had been flagging for most of the afternoon and it tore Mina's heart to think that she was causing distress to the beautiful animal. She took time to rub down her sides and stroke her flank before settling her at the side of the clearing where there was fresh green grass for her to graze on.

Arion had just started to build a fire pit when he froze, listening.

Mina cocked her head and tried to figure out what he was hearing but all she could make out was a light breeze through the trees. Then it occurred to her. That was *all* she could hear. Earlier the forest was alive with sounds of birds and small animals. Now it was silent except for the wind. A shiver raced down her spine and her hand went for the small dagger that she'd taken to carrying in her belt.

The horses began to grow restless. Mina moved to calm her mare but the animal snorted and rolled her eyes nervously, side stepping as if from an invisible enemy. Mina tried to soothe her but both mounts were seriously spooked.

"Arion?" she asked uncertainly.

"Sshhh." He put his finger to his lip and was moving toward her when the first black shadow whirled into the clearing.

Mina's mare screamed and reared, ripping her tether from the ground as she ran into the forest.

Mina stood paralyzed in front of the creature. She watched in horror as it lifted its hands toward her, preparing to attack her just as had happened the previous year. Mina was powerless to do anything. She vaguely realized the dagger had fallen from her fingertips as she encountered the red gaze of the creature in front of her.

But before the terrible sucking sensation started, the creature's head disconnected from its body and it crumpled revealing Arion behind it, his sword dripping red with blood.

Mina took a step toward him but before she could reach him two more Hunters materialized. One was armed and slashed at Arion with a dagger. Mina cried out when she saw his tunic turn red where the blade had connected with his shoulder but Arion didn't hesitate. He whirled around carrying his sword with him and sliced the creature in two. Mina had never seen anything like Arion when he fought. It was almost as though he was dancing, his grace and balance unmatched even by the Hunters.

The third Hunter's attention was on Mina. He'd separated her from Arion and was approaching her, his mouth stretched grotesquely in a smile that revealed pointed teeth.

"You are mine now," he hissed at her. But suddenly Arion was between her and the creature.

He snarled something at the Hunter in Elder language and began attacking with his sword.

Mina was dismayed by the amount of blood that had seeped through Arion's shirt but he seemed to not feel it. He continued sparring with the creature, keeping Mina out of its reach.

Then with a sudden yell, Arion lunched at the creature and embedded his sword so deeply through its middle that the blade penetrated through the creature's back. Mina closed her eyes as she heard the wet sucking sound as Arion removed his sword from the Hunter's body.

"Princess Minathrial, are you hurt?" he asked.

Mina opened her eyes, forcing her fear back. "No," she said softly, her gaze catching on the growing crimson stain on Arion's tunic. She shook her head. "I'm not but you are, Arion."

She gestured to his shirt; the entire sleeve was now saturated in dark red blood.

Arion looked to where she pointed and seemed surprised to see his own blood.

"We must get the horses and leave this place."

But Mina shook her head. "Not until we see the extent of your injury. That's a lot of blood, Arion," she said faintly.

He looked about to argue but Mina held his gaze. It would be ridiculous to even attempt to ride when one was bleeding so copiously. And if Arion died there would be no one to protect her. His thoughts seemed to echo her own and he sat, resigned to the circumstances.

Mina hurried over to her saddlebags to find the medical supplies Thia had packed for her. "Take off your shirt and we'll see how bad the damage is," she said over her shoulder as she located the supplies she needed. "Brijit and Thia might be the most gifted healers in our family but I learned a thing or two about treating injuries."

She looked up and saw Arion rooted to the same spot as she left him, his shirtsleeve still dripping with blood and his face pale.

"Arion, you must remove your shirt," she repeated.

Still he did nothing. He just stared at Mina.

What was wrong with him? Was he in shock? Could the injury be more serious than she first thought? Worried she walked back to where he stood and reached a hand to the hem of his shirt. Suddenly he flinched away.

"I can't treat the injury until I see it, Arion," she said impatiently.

He clenched his jaw and for a moment just stared at her. Finally he spoke. "A princess should not have to see this."

Mina shook her head. "Perhaps but I wasn't raised a princess. I was raised a small village girl and I've treated plenty of injuries when my mother and sister were otherwise occupied."

"I'm not talking about my injury," Arion said so softly Mina almost missed it.

Suddenly she remembered his disfigurement. Arion didn't want her to see his scars. What did she imagine she would do at the sight of them? She wasn't some weak stomached girl who would wilt away. He was being ridiculous!

"Arion if you die, I will be alone. How long do you think I will survive with these-" She gestured to the dead bodies of the Hunters on the ground in the clearing, "trailing me?"

Arion said nothing. But after a few minutes of silence he reached for the hem of his shirt, his eyes on her face.

Mina was careful to keep her face blank of all emotion but even she was not prepared for the sight of Arion's scars. She'd seen the damaged skin that crept up the one side of his neck but what she didn't expect was that it would be so extensive. The skin was discolored and roped, puckering in angry thick lines across his chest, shoulders and back. After the first revelation, Mina kept her eyes carefully trained on the stab wound, which was on his upper shoulder.

She licked her lips. The wound was bleeding extensively but she couldn't tell how bad it was yet. She reached for her canteen and poured water over it.

Arion hissed.

"I'm sorry," she whispered. "I need to clean it and see how deep it is."

As the water sluiced away, Mina was relieved to see that it was a superficial wound after all. She reached into the medical supplies satchel and spread a balm Thia had prepared over the clean wound. Then she took out some linen bandages and began to wrap the wound.

"It's bleeding a lot but it's not too deep. I think you'll survive," she said with a small smile.

Arion kept silent the entire time, his mouth tight. When Mina finally finished the task she looked up at him and found him watching her, an expression of humiliation on his face.

"Arion," she said softly, impulsively reaching out and touching his cheek.

He stood suddenly and moved away, his gaze on the tree line. "We need to find the horses and get away from here."

"Do you have a clean shirt?" Mina asked.

He nodded and went over to his saddlebags, digging through them until he pulled out a white linen shirt and pulled it over his head.

Mina watched him as he turned from her. His scars were horrifying but not in the way he thought. They were shocking because his mother had done this to him. Someone he had loved and trusted had betrayed him in the most heinous way possible. But she didn't think Arion could understand that. Or perhaps he didn't want to examine it too closely.

#

Despite Mina's protests that he needed to rest, Arion insisted on locating their horses and continuing the journey.

"Arion, you've lost a lot of blood and suffered a trauma. Don't you think you should take some time to recover at least a little?" Mina asked as she followed him into the forest looking for their horses.

He stopped abruptly and turned to her.

"Three Hunters in one place, Minathrial? Three! That means they are sensing you and we need to move on." The only sign of his agitation was the fact that he'd dropped the title of princess when he spoke to her. He whistled for the horses but there was no sign of them.

"Do you think we can outrun them?" Mina asked, fear making her voice shake. "They teleported here."

Arion was silent for a few minutes. The forest had returned to its normal sounds. He whistled again and waited.

A few moments later there was a soft nicker and Mina saw both their horses coming back through the trees. But when they led them back to the clearing, her mare became skittish and spooked.

"They don't like the bodies of the Hunters," Arion observed as he gathered up their supplies.

"If you hold the horses, I can do that." Mina insisted, worried that he'd start his wound bleeding again but Arion ignored her. And in a few short minutes they were both mounted and leaving the clearing.

Mina looked back at the three broken bodies and shuddered. They didn't have time to bury them, which meant anyone who came this way would stumble upon them. But it was a little travelled road so it was likely that the bodies wouldn't be discovered for a very long time.

Arion spoke again as they cantered North. "You're right about one thing," he conceded.

"What's that?" Mina asked.

He looked ahead. "More of them are sure to sense you and I don't know how many more attacks like that I can win."

Mina swallowed her fear but looked ahead miserably remembering the terror she'd felt as the one Hunter had advanced on her. She could only imagine how scared she would have been if Arion not been there. And the thought of Arion dying filled her with a sadness that she couldn't explain. It was as if she already couldn't imagine her life without him.

"Do you have any idea for keeping us safe?" she asked, shifting her thoughts away from dangerous revelations.

He smiled slightly. "Actually you gave me one." She looked at him questioningly.

"You mentioned that you'd been safe in Sailsburg."

She nodded. "We never even saw a Hunter while we were there."

"Well, I don't know if we will make it safely to the Refuge on our own. And Xyrisse said that whatever it is that attracts the Hunters is wearing off. Who knows how long it will be until you can't be detected at all? Or at least anymore than any Marked One can be sensed. Once that happens it will be safe to travel. But for now our best plan to achieve safety is to hide in numbers."

Mina didn't understand. How could they do that when there was just the two of them? As if reading her mind Arion explained.

"Find a city to hide in," he smiled grimly. "And I know one that's less than two day's journey from here. Bermgarten should be our destination. And even better we can stay with Helpers."

#

They had no more trouble from Hunters in the three days it took to arrive in Bermgarten. Even though the city was close to the clearing where they were attacked, Arion was not able to ride for as long as he normally did. On the evening of the second day North, Mina looked at Arion across from the fire from her. For the first time he looked tired. Lines of exhaustion were carved into his cheeks and she wondered if he'd slept at all since the attack. She could also guess that he was in a fair bit of pain from his injury.

"You know I should be changing that bandage and having a look at your wound," she told him, after observing him for a few minutes, wondering if he was developing an infection.

He grunted in reply.

"Arion, don't be a baby. Your wound needs to be cleaned and checked." She stood up to move toward him but he flinched away from her. "I promise I'll be careful," she said softly as she sat down behind him waiting for him to remove his shirt.

He stayed sitting unmoving in front of her.

She reached forward and pretended not to notice when he pulled away from her touch.

"Once was enough, Princess," he said gruffly.

Mina sighed in exacerbation. What was wrong with men? Clearly he was in pain and she was concerned about his shoulder. At the very least he needed the bandage changed.

"Arion, you are being ridiculous. Do you want infection to set in? How will you be able to protect me if that happens?"

He stared into the fire and ignored her. Mina bit her cheek and counted to ten in her head, determined to wait him out.

After a few minutes, he shrugged grudgingly and began to unbutton his shirt. Mina smiled to herself. Perhaps patience was the best way to get through to Arion.

She carefully untied his bandage. His wound was swollen and red but there was no sign of infection. Mina breathed a sigh of relief as she cleaned it out with water again and used some of Thia's herbal salve to dress it. Once again Arion flinched when she poured the water over the wound.

"I'm sorry," she whispered and began to bandage it again. "It looks good."

"I told you it was fine," he said gruffly.

Mina shook her head. Arion would not say thank you, it seemed. As she finished the bandages she looked at the scars on his back. Although they were old, she could see that they must still cause him discomfort. They were stretched and ridged over the heavy muscles on his back. Impulsively she reached out and traced a particularly puckered spot.

Arion rose to his feet immediately and walked across their campsite. Mina silently cursed herself. Just when he was starting to feel, if not comfortable, at least less guarded with her.

"I'm sorry," she called again.

He didn't answer so she stayed silent as he put his shirt on and began to button it. He kept his back to her so she couldn't see his face and she wondered what he was thinking.

Finally he turned around to face her. Mina was surprised by the raw anger that blazed in his eyes.

"Don't ever touch me again," he said.

Mina flinched. "I'm sorry," she whispered for the third time. "I just thought it must cause you discomfort at times …"

Arion stood in the shadows, staying far from her.

"You know, the scars aren't as bad as you think they are, Arion." She stood and moved to where her sleeping roll was laid out on the ground. "At least your physical scars aren't."

With that parting shot, she slipped into her roll and tried to sleep.

Arion didn't move for a long while; she could feel him watching her. Finally he returned to the fire. Mina rolled over and to her surprise fell into a deep slumber.

CHAPTER TWELVE

They'd been at the Refuge less than 24 hours when Kiara was summoned to Bellasiel's chamber. Annoyed at having her plans for the day interrupted, Kiara considered ignoring the Elder's request. Bellasiel had been acting as if she were the commander of the Refuge, expecting everyone to do her bidding. It rubbed Kiara the wrong way.

But she grudgingly put her plans on hold to see what the Elder wanted. Kiara had planned to check on the training of the Marked Ones that had been at the Refuge all summer and then she was going to find Caedmon. Although he'd left under the pretense of trying to come up with a way to help Teague, she couldn't shake the feeling that he was angry with her. She wanted to find him and make sure she knew where his emotions lay. But the summons from Bellasiel changed all her plans. And to ignore Bellasiel would probably end up causing her more trouble that it was worth.

When Kiara arrived in Bellasiel's chamber she saw the Elder was not alone. She had Deanna with her. Kiara's stomach tightened in to a knot. Obviously the Elder had discovered that one of the children Kiara had brought back to the Refuge was not Marked.

"Kiara," Bellasiel nodded in greeting. "Are you aware that one of the children you brought here is not Marked?" Her words echoed Kiara's thoughts and the Elder's pale eyes couldn't have been more ice-laced.

Deanna was sitting on a wooden chair in the corner of the chamber watching Bellasiel with large frightened eyes. Kiara felt a stab of annoyance. Why did Bellasiel have to drag Deanna in here and scare her? Couldn't she have just questioned Kiara on her own? After the poor girl had lived with a tyrannical mother for her short life, she could only imagine what the Elder's dominating presence was doing to Deanna. But swallowing her anger, Kiara forced herself to nod in response.

"Can you explain why you would bring a child who does not bear the Mark to us?" Bellasiel pressed, her expression hard and watchful.

"Deanna's mother tried to pawn her off on us as a Marked child. She'd drawn a rudimentary Mark on her right shoulder," Kiara explained.

Bellasiel interrupted, "And so what? If you discovered that the Mark was not genuine why did you not return her to her family?"

Kiara looked at the pitiful girl in the corner, Deanna was close to tears and looked terrified of Bellasiel. Her anger sparked.

"She needed help and there was no one else to give it to her."

"That may have been true but we don't offer charity to just anyone in need, we can't afford to," Bellasiel insisted. "The Refuge is not a hideaway for every needy child in the Five Corners. We can't be that even if we wanted to."

Kiara looked at Bellasiel levelly. On a rational level she knew Bellasiel was right – Caedmon has said the same thing – but something about the Elder's manner was just rubbing Kiara the wrong way. "I know that," she finally admitted stonily.

Bellasiel nodded as if everything was settled. "Good. Then we'll send her back to where she came from."

"No!" Deanna cried in terror. She ran across the room to hide behind Kiara's legs.

"I will not send her back," Kiara said firmly. "I made the decision to bring her here and I won't go back on it."

Bellasiel's eyes narrowed. "What good is she here? She isn't Marked so can't train. She is just another mouth to feed. Come winter we will not have the resources to feed extra mouths, Kiara. With the drought worsening we have precious little to share now."

"I will feed her myself," Kiara said.

"How?" Bellasiel questioned. "By taking food from others' mouths?"

"No," Kiara answered evenly, "I can hunt and find food in the mountains."

But Bellasiel was shaking her head. "We can't afford to have you traipsing through the mountains. You are needed here."

Kiara lifted her chin. She would not send Deanna back to the horrible existence she'd rescued her from. Kiara remembered all too clearly the hatred the child's mother had thrown her way.

"Sending her back would not be in her best interests," Kiara said firmly. "She stays. I will share my rations with her and she can sleep in my room if you have no bed for her but I will not send her back. If you make her leave, I will go as well."

Kiara knew they couldn't afford to lose her, especially with her sisters not having arrived yet and with the troubles with Teague and Caedmon.

Bellasiel tapped her index finger against her mouth studying Kiara and the girl for a few minutes.

"Does she have any useful skills, at least?" Bellasiel asked finally. Kiara felt a thrill of relief go through her. She was worried that Bellasiel would call her bluff and have Deanna removed from the Refuge.

"I don't know," Kiara admitted. Then she remembered all the younger children in Deanna's house. There were sure to be some skills the girl would have had to learn in order to survive in such an environment. She kneeled down in front of her. "Deanna, what can you do that's useful?"

The little girl looked down at her feet then looked up at Kiara doubtfully.

"You want to be useful here, don't you? We all must do some kind of work. I would be so happy if you could tell us how you could help."

Deanna swallowed and then nodded. "Ma made me cook, although I don't think I'm very good at it," she admitted shyly. "And I had to keep the young'uns quiet less I got walloped from Ma. So I 'spose I got pretty good at that." She braved a glance in Bellasiel's direction. "I know how to keep real quiet so I won't be seen or heard. I got good at that, too," she admitted.

Bellasiel leaned forward at the last statement. "How good?" she asked suddenly. "Child, how good were you at not being seen?"

Kiara didn't like the eager gleam in Bellasiel's eyes. But Deanna answered her steadily. "Real good. Ma would beat us real bad if she knew we was there. 'Specially if she'd been in the gin. I got real good at it else I might have ended up like Tommy-Rae."

"What happened to Tommy-Rae?" Kiara asked, a sick, uneasy feeling in her stomach.

"Ma walloped him so hard cross the head with her iron, his skull cracked open and he dropped down dead right then and there."

Kiara stared at Deanna in horror. How could a parent do that to her own child? And what's more, Deanna was recounting it so passively, as if it was just part of life. Kiara felt a sudden flood of relief that she'd got Deanna out of that home.

But Bellasiel was smiling ever so slightly as if Deanna's story had peaked her interest in the girl. "What is your name, child?" she asked.

"Deanna."

"Deanna, I think we may have a use for you after all." She looked satisfied and Kiara didn't like it. What was Bellasiel up to now? "Kiara, take Deanna down to the barracks where the other children sleep. Find her a bed and some clean clothes. Then after she's had something to eat, you can start."

Kiara looked at Bellasiel sharply. "Start what?" she asked.

"Start training your little friend to be a spy."

#

"Did you sleep in the dorms last night?" Kiara asked Deanna, being careful to keep her tone as neutral as possible and not betrayal the anger that was threatening to erupt at Bellasiel's last words.

The little girl nodded trustingly.

"Okay, go back down there and I'll come find you soon. I need to speak to Bellasiel."

The little girl darted a nervous look in the Elder's direction and then hurried toward the door. Kiara waited until she heard the door close and the pitter patter of Deana's feet running in the opposite direction before she turned to Bellasiel.

"She is just a child," Kiara said, anger making her voice rough.

"They are all children, Kiara," Bellasiel said calmly as she turned to some scrolls on her desk, effectively dismissing her.

"Yes, they are. So why are you treating them as if they are pawns in a game?" Kiara paced the floor. "I thought we were bringing these children to safety, not setting them up to be trained as … as what?" She remembered Teague's frenzied words and Caedmon's growing suspicions. "An army?"

Bellasiel poured herself a cup of tea and observed Kiara over the rim of her mug. "They need to learn to defend themselves," she said blandly. "You, of all people, should know that."

Kiara shook her head in frustration. "Yes. Defend themselves but from what I saw yesterday, you're teaching them a lot more than defensive moves."

"We don't know what they will be up against in the long run."

"And what are your plans for Deanna? You're training her to be a spy at age six?" Kiara shook her head remembering how horrified her sisters and she had been when they realized that Caedmon and Teague had been sent off for training in their respective careers at that age. She thought the Refuge was going to be different than the rest of the Five Corners but it seemed as though Bellasiel was doing the same thing as the Army and *Draíodóir* had always done. "They should have a chance to be children."

Bellasiel looked up, her gaze hard. To Kiara's surprise, she nodded. "Yes, you're right, Kiara. They *should* have a chance to be children but they've had the misfortune to be born with a Mark that denies them the luxury."

Kiara laughed bitterly. "You're saying childhood is a luxury?"

"For some it is," Bellasiel acknowledged coldly. "These children will not have mothers and fathers to care for them. They need to learn to care for themselves and each other. You and Caedmon can help them to do that. Or you can focus on one child - one who isn't even Marked -and ignore the others."

"That's not what I was suggesting," Kiara protested, not liking the way Bellasiel was speaking about the Marked Ones. As if they were different than other children.

"Good. Then we are in agreement. I recommend you use your considerable skill set to help all the children we have here. They will get used to the living conditions and their homesickness will fade. Those are not your concerns. These children, even that unmarked one you've adopted to *The Cause*, can learn much from you. I suspect your little Deanna can teach the others a lot about survival."

Kiara couldn't argue with that. She had a feeling that Deanna's entire live had revolved around learning to survive. But she didn't like how Bellasiel was now talking about a "cause." There had been no such talk when they'd followed her from Séreméla to the Refuge. Kiara suddenly had a strong sense that Teague's suspicions might be right.

"I believe that everything happens for a reason, Kiara. You didn't stumble upon that little girl by accident. There is a reason you found her. And her knowledge may be it. She is here for a reason, of that I'm certain."

Kiara felt a shiver run down her spine at the tone in Bellasiel's voice. She sounded almost mystical, as if she was utterly convinced that there was some kind of predestination to their lives. Kiara studied the Elder steadily. She'd never noticed the harshness around the woman's mouth before. Still Bellasiel was right in a lot of what she was saying, even if Kiara didn't like it.

Finding Refuge

Finally Kiara turned and left the chamber. She needed to find Caedmon and see if he could help her make sense of what Bellasiel had told her.

CHAPTER THIRTEEN

Kiara found Caedmon as he left Teague's room. She noted the lines of fatigue around his eyes with concern and she wondered if he'd slept at all the previous night.

"How is he?" she asked even though she could tell her question was rhetorical.

Caedmon ran his hand over his face and shook his head. "Walk with me. I need some air."

Kiara followed him as he climbed through the dark, steep passageway, up to the entrance of the Refuge. As they emerged from the Refuge, Kiara took a deep breath of the late summer air. The Eastern Mountains weren't as harsh, weather-wise, as the Northern Mountains but the jagged peaks and grey rocks were not inviting. Nonetheless, after being in the mine the fresh air made the mountain passageways seem almost homey.

A warm breeze lifted the hair on Kiara's neck. She'd continued to let her hair grow despite her usual practice of keeping it sheared close to her head. Caedmon never told her what he thought of her hair but she'd noticed that he liked to run his fingers through her locks when he was distracted. So she'd continued to grow it for him and she found that she was starting to enjoy the sensation of having hair again. She couldn't imagine caring for hair as long as Mina's blond waves but her short style she could handle. And if she were honest, it made her feel more feminine.

Caedmon led her to a large flat rock that was big enough for both of them to sit on.

"Did you sleep at all?" Kiara asked, his fatigue even more obvious in daylight.

Caedmon shook his head. "I've moved into Teague's room." He ran his hand over his unshaven cheeks once more and looked unseeingly across the meadow in front of them. "He's bad, Kiara. I'm starting to think that his mind has been permanently damaged."

Kiara stared at him. Dismay welled up inside her. Even though she had warned Caedmon that something was wrong with his brother, deep down she hadn't believed that he could be permanently damaged.

"Maybe Bellasiel and Omen are right about the *Draíodóir* slowly corrupting his mind." The despair in Caedmon's voice made Kiara's heart twinge painfully. She put her head on his shoulder and gave him a hug as she tried to think of a way she could tell him about her own fears concerning Bellasiel.

Kiara licked her lips. "Or …" Caedmon down looked at her. She took a deep breath. "Maybe Teague is right about Bellasiel."

Caedmon furrowed his brow in confusion. "What do you mean?"

Kiara sighed. She knew that this was going against everything she'd argued with him about the previous day but her feelings about Bellasiel were starting to change. She told Caedmon about her conversation with Bellasiel that morning and the doubts that had started to creep into her mind.

"I told you we should have left that girl. We can't waste time or resources on all the unwanted children in the Five Corners, this place would be overrun."

Irritation pricked at the back of her mind. Caedmon was missing the point of what she'd told him, fixating on Deanna again. Kiara nodded impatiently. "I know. I know. It wasn't just that Bellasiel was complaining about Deanna. It was …" she paused searching for the words to explain the uneasy feeling that was growing in the pit of her stomach. Then she shook her head. "The way she talked about the Marked Ones, it's as if they are things not people." She looked at Caedmon. "And we are Marked Ones, too. Does she think we've forgotten that?"

Caedmon didn't reply instead he focused on the vista in front of them again.

"I guess I don't have a good reason for suspecting ill of her and perhaps if Teague hadn't said anything I wouldn't have been suspicious but I just have this feeling. I don't know how much we can trust her. And remember Meldiron said the only ones we can trust are other Marked Ones."

Caedmon focused his dark eyes on her again. "That was before we knew about Bellasiel and the sympathizers, Kiara. They have put so much into helping us. How can we truly doubt them?"

He did have a point. But Kiara could shake the suspicions that were prodding her. "I know. But there's another thing that worries me.

Look at this place, Caedmon." She sat up straight and gestured towards the mine behind them. "How long do you think it took to prepare this Refuge? We're not talking about a few weeks or even months. This would have taken years to build. And to organize all the people working here and all the Helpers?" She shook her head. "Clearly this had been in the works for a long time. Obviously Bellasiel and the others knew we weren't the only Marked Ones," she laughed mirthlessly. "Why else would they have created such a large place for us? It means that Brijit and the others knew the entire time that there were others. But they sure didn't tell us that, did they?"

Kiara remembered how her mother, Brijit, had let the girls believe they were special for most of their lives and suddenly her feelings were mixed into an unreadable mess, like a pile of paints spilled over the ground. Brijit had kept so many truths from Kiara and her sisters and yet … Kiara remembered her mother lying in her lap, dying. She blinked back her tears. Brijit loved them right to the end. Nothing that happened could change that. But the lies still stung. Kiara felt Caedmon's arm suddenly around her, pulling her back until her head was on his shoulder again.

"How many lies did they tell us, Caedmon?" she sniffled trying to hold back the tears.

Caedmon didn't answer her but Kiara didn't expect him to. Their relationship was like that. He listened to her and only spoke when he needed to. Often it was like they communicated on a level where words weren't necessary. They sat for a long time in the warm sun until Caedmon stood up and held out his hand to pull her to standing.

He stared down at her as if he were trying to figure out how to say what was on his mind. "I have a favor to ask of you, Kiara."

She looked up at him, wondering what he needed.

"I need you to look after Teague for me."

"Why?" Kiara asked, confused. Caedmon had moved into Teague's room. What more could she do?

"I have some business to take care of that will take me away from here," he said evasively and Kiara noticed that he suddenly wasn't meeting her eyes.

Fear prickled along her skin. Caedmon and her did not keep secrets. Why was he suddenly so standoffish. "What kind of business?" she asked.

Caedmon turned his gaze to meet hers. "Please don't ask, Kee. I can't answer. Just trust me on this one. It's necessary and might provide us with a few answers as to what is going on here."

She didn't see why he couldn't tell her what he was up to. Kiara opened her mouth to argue.

"And please, don't argue," he said, gently covering her lips with his finger. "I don't have the energy today."

Kiara looked at his tired, handsome face and her heart melted a little. And she hated herself for it. Caedmon was her weakness.

"You know me too well," Kiara said irritably. "Okay. I won't ask what business you are up to. But I will ask why I can't come with you, Caedmon? We make a good team. You could use my help."

He shook his head sadly. "Not this time. I need you here guarding Teague."

"Guarding him?" Kiara frowned at his choice of words. "Do you think he's in danger?"

Caedmon's face hardened. "If what you say is true then he is in more danger than we can imagine," he admitted. "I need you to do this for me, Kiara. Stay with him and keep Omen away from him." Caedmon had never trusted the old *Draíodóir* but he had believed he was helping Teague until now.

Kiara was surprised. Omen was supposed to be helping Teague break his link with the *Draíodóir*. "Do you think he means Teague harm?" she asked, worry suddenly making her feel a bit ill. Omen had been given free access to Teague. If he actually was harming him instead of helping him ... Kiara closed her eyes. She didn't want to think of what it could mean.

Caedmon stood and turned toward the entrance to the mine. "I don't know," he admitted as they started walking. "But Teague becomes almost irrational when Omen is around. It's clearly not good for him to be with that *Draíodóir*."

"Former *Draíodóir*," Kiara reminded him softly but Caedmon pressed his lips together and did not reply. Kiara wondered if Caedmon's choice of words were not unintentional. Could it be that he suspected Omen still worked for the *Draíodóir?*

"When do you have to leave?" Kiara asked, hoping he would delay for a while so she could try to learn more of what his suspicions might be.

"Tomorrow morning," he said. Then he stopped and pulled her into his arms. "Thank you!" He whispered before he lowered his lips to hers.

Kiara sighed into the kiss. It had been so long since Caedmon had shown any affection toward her. But too soon he was pulling away, albeit a bit reluctantly.

She watched him head toward Teague's chamber and hoped that they were both wrong about Bellasiel and Omen. More than anything Kiara wished that the Elder was on their side and not another distrustful enemy they had to watch out for. If she wasn't what she appeared to be, who would be left for them to trust in the Five Corners?

#

Caedmon left before Kiara was even awake the next morning. She went to Teague's chambers hoping to say goodbye to him but to her dismay she only found Teague there. She tried to hide her disappointment from Teague.

"Has Caedmon left?" she asked, looking at Teague closely and suddenly noticing the grey hue to his skin.

Teague nodded despondently. "I know Caedmon told you to keep an eye on me, Kiara, but you don't have to."

Kiara tried to catch Teague's gaze but his eyes rarely stayed focused on any one spot for anything length of time. They would flit from one object in the room to another almost constantly. This was so different from the playful and happy Teague who'd been quick to befriend everyone back at the Inn.

And he wouldn't meet her eyes. Instead he looked at her ear, her elbow, her feet, her left hand and then the bed frame, his shirt, and so on. It was almost as though his mind was cycling through the different things in the room, trying to find an anchor to focus on but unable to do so.

"Teague," Kiara said gently but his eyes didn't stop their roaming and his hands were shaking ever so slightly. "Teague, when did you sleep last?"

He stood up and started pacing the room. "Sleep? I've not been able to sleep for weeks. I don't remember. Ever since Omen's last session with me."

A chill ran down Kiara's back. "Have you spoken to Thia?" she asked.

Teague's silver eyes suddenly focused on her own. "Thia!" he exclaimed with deep despair.

Kiara watched him closely as tears filled his eyes. Teague was obviously exhausted and miserable. It was almost as if he were a torture victim. Without thinking Kiara crossed the room and put her arms around him. She felt him wilt in her embrace and his raw sobs filled the room.

Kiara remembered Teague as a fun-loving sweet guy and here he was reduced to this shell of his former self. She shook her head. After a few minutes he calmed down and Kiara led him over to the bed in the corner of the room.

"Lie down, surely you can rest even if you can't sleep," she told him.

When he'd climbed into the bed and she'd tucked him in almost as if he were a small child, Kiara sat on the edge of the bed.

"Do you remember when you did see Thia last?"

Teague sniffled and seemed to consider her question. "It was a while ago. Maybe three weeks," he said softly.

Kiara nodded. "And did she say where she was or what was happening then?"

He shook his head. "They were still in Sailsburg but she said she would talk to Meldiron about leaving." Teague looked guilty suddenly.

"What's wrong?" Kiara asked.

"I got a bit upset. It was starting to become too much to deal with alone and I needed Thia here. She's the only one who really understands me." He paused, his eyes filling with tears again. "We had a fight. She said I was being unreasonable and maybe I was. I just wanted her to get here."

Kiara nodded in understanding but didn't press Teague for details. She missed her sisters as well. They'd been gone far too long. She knew that Meldiron was determined to locate his friend but she wondered if it wasn't just a lost cause given how long Arion had been missing. If she was honest she was starting to worry about the delay in their arrival at the Refuge. The Hunters were looking for all Marked Ones and that included Thia and Mina. But there was no point in worrying Teague. The last thing he needed was more stress.

"Thia isn't likely to take your bad humor the wrong way, Teague," Kiara assured him. "Remember she grew up with me and I'm a famous for my temper. Don't worry, I know they've been delayed but look at how long overdue we all were arriving at Séreméla. I'm sure they are well. There are lots of factors that could delay an expedition south."

Teague didn't look convinced and, if she were honest, Kiara had to admit that she wasn't confident of her sisters' safety either. But Teague was worked up enough, it wouldn't do to have him worry more.

"Why don't you try to rest?" Kiara suggested. "I'll stay right here with you. I promise."

#

Teague didn't sleep but he did rest. As she'd promised to do, Kiara stayed with him all day.

In the afternoon there was a knock at the door and Teague's restfulness was over. She'd never seen him react so violently to anything. He sprung from the bed and cowered in the corner.

Kiara looked at the door in confusion. How could a knock on the door upset him so much?

"It's Omen," he said shrilly. "He's coming for me."

"Teague, it's alright. I won't let him hurt you," Kiara assured him, concerned by his reaction.

When she opened the door she saw that Teague was right. It was the former *Draíodóir* apprentice who claimed to be helping Teague. Kiara had never liked the man. He was short with a bald head and beady eyes of a colorless hue. And he always had the semblance of a smirk around the corners of his small mouth.

He was clearly surprised to see Kiara. "Miss Kiara, I didn't realize you were back," he said in a casual tone that did nothing to hide his obvious lie.

He made her skin crawl. Kiara knew he was well informed that Caedmon and her had returned. Bellasiel had told her so. But he clearly had no qualms about lying through his teeth.

"I'm here to work with Teague," he told her importantly. 'We have lots of work to do if we are to keep him safe, you know," he added with a smile that didn't reach his eyes. This man was insincerity embodied.

Kiara straightened to her full height, towering over the small man. "Teague is indisposed today," she told him.

"He's indisposed because our work has been delayed for the last few weeks," Omen shot back at her, his tone resonating with self-importance.

"I don't think that's the reason at all," Kiara said coldly not letting the man step even a foot into the room. "Teague needs to rest today. You can talk to me about when you can work with him again. Once he's recovered his strength."

Omen looked like he was about to argue but then he seemed to think better of it.

"As you wish, Miss Kiara," he said smoothly and bowed to her. "I will return when Teague is well. Tell him that I was here, will you? And let him know that I only have his well-being in mind."

Kiara stood and watched as the man disappeared down the corridor. Odious toad, she thought to herself. He was lying through his teeth and it practically killed him that she'd sent him away. She turned back to see Teague muttering to himself by the wall and her heart sank. He'd seemed so much more relaxed after resting all day and now he was worse than ever.

"Teague, it's okay, he's gone." But Teague didn't respond to her. Despair wash over her as she realized how fragile his mind was. She looked around the room and saw a bed tucked in the corner opposite from Teague's. Cademon's sweater was on the foot of it.

"I'm staying here with you tonight, Teague. You don't have to worry, I won't leave you."

Later that night as Kiara turned the lamps off and settled into the bed she could still hear Teague muttering to himself. He seemed to have no idea that she was in the room with him. Kiara sighed and climbed into Caedmon's bed, pulling the blankets up to her chin and breathing in his scent.

She wondered where Caedmon had gone and what he hoped to discover. It wasn't like him to keep secrets from her. He was normally very open with her. In fact, she could only remember one topic he didn't like to discuss. Kiara's heart began to beat harder.

Caedmon never spoke of his past with the Army. In fact she knew almost nothing about his time in the Army or how he came to leave it. The fact that he left was extraordinary in itself.

In the Five Corners being a soldier was a life long commitment. Soldiers did not have wives or families. Once they joined the ranks, they didn't leave until they died. Retirement was not an issue – few soldiers lived into old age and those that did, continued to live with the Army.

If Caedmon was returning to the Army seeking information, he could be putting himself in danger. Deserter soldiers, while rare, were killed if they ever returned.

Kiara rolled over on the bed and closed her eyes, blocking out the negative nature of her thoughts. Caedmon would not take unnecessary risks. He was careful and calculated in all his decisions. She had to believe that this case was no exception and that he would return to them soon.

#

The next morning Teague seemed to be himself again.

"You really didn't need to stay here, Kiara," he told her with a smile, the first one she'd seen on his face since she'd arrived.

"Well, I thought you might want to talk in the night and you shouldn't be alone," she told him not wanting to share with him how frightened she'd been of his incomprehensible ramblings before she fell asleep.

"That was kind of you," he said and sat down to the small table where Kiara has set the breakfast that had been delivered to them earlier. She was pleased to see Teague taking an interest in food even if it was just a passing fancy.

"So what are your plans for today?" she asked him with a smile.

But before Teague could reply there was a soft knock at the door. Kiara looked at him but he seemed undisturbed by the interruption. Not Omen then.

Still Kiara kept her dagger within reach when she opened the door. On the other side was Deanna, looking uncertain and a bit scared.

"Deanna! What are you doing here?" Kiara asked as she beckoned for her to come in.

Deanna stepped over the threshold hesitantly. She looked at Teague and then down at her feet.

"Well?" Kiara prodded when the girl seemed to have lost her ability to speak.

"You're needed in the training chamber," she whispered.

Kiara raised her eyebrows in surprise. "What do you mean I'm needed, Deanna?"

"Them kids you brung here are arguing and fighting. They won't listen to no one. That Elder lady told me to come and get you to see if you can do sumthink about it."

Kiara looked at Teague reluctantly.

"Go," he said with a smile as he took a large bite of a biscuit with fruit preserves spread on it. "Really, Kiara, you don't need to stay here and keep me company."

Still Kiara hesitated. She had a bad feeling about this.

"Please, Miss, I'm scared the kids are gonna really hurt each other. They got them weapons that that man was showing them how to use."

"What man?" Kiara asked suddenly,

The girl shrugged. "I don't know his name. He's got no hair and he's not very big."

Omen. Kiara hurried to the door. What was he doing interfering with the training? Hadn't he caused enough trouble with Teague?

"I won't be long," she told Teague before she stepped out.

He shrugged unconcerned. "Take your time. I'm not going anywhere."

Kiara watched him for a moment longer then impulsively turned to Deanna. "Deanna, this is my friend Teague. He's been quite ill lately but he won't let anyone help him too much. Do you think you could stay with him?"

Deanna nodded eagerly, wanting to please Kiara.

"Teague, Deanna will stay and keep you company."

Teague looked at the little girl and smiled. "Hmm, I wish I had my mandolin - we could sing together, Deanna. But do you know how to play back hand?"

The little girl nodded eagerly.

"Okay. We'll have a back hand tournament, just you and me. But I haven't played in a long time so you need to take it a bit easy on me."

Kiara watched them for a moment longer, unable to shake the little voice that was telling her she should stay. But Teague's curly head was bent beside Deanna's dark one as he discussed the merits of the game with Deanna. He sounded just like the happy-go-lucky Teague she'd known at the Inn and Kiara forced herself to turn away.

After all what could possibly happen?

#

Kiara arrived at the training chamber to find it full of children cooperating and listening intently to their instructor who, like Caedmon, was a former member of the army. There was no sign of any disruption at all in the room.

Kiara turned realizing she'd been duped, only to run straight into Bellasiel.

"Ah, Kiara, you've come to help with the children's training. Good, we could use your assistance since Caedmon has disappeared."

Bellasiel paused and looked at her closely. "You don't happen to know where he's gone do you?"

Kiara looked at the exit to the room and realized that she would have to stay for a while now. She'd clearly been tricked into leaving Teague. Which meant that Teague was possibly in danger. Or it could just mean that Omen wanted to spend time with him. She just hoped that having Deanna with him might help.

She turned to Bellasiel. "He didn't tell me where he was going. I think he just needed to run a few errands." She looked at the exit trying to think of an excuse to leave.

Bellasiel narrowed her eyes. "You know if you need anything we can always get it for you."

Kiara looked at the Elder sharply. Clearly Bellasiel was not good with them coming and going whenever they pleased. It became clear to Kiara once again that Bellasiel saw herself as a kind of commander in the Refuge. As long as they fell in line with what she wanted she let them believe that they were free but was it possible that they were not? Her stomach cramped at the thought.

Kiara turned back toward the group of children training. "Well, I'd better see where I can help out," she said agreeably, hoping that Bellasiel would move on and Kiara could then return to Teague.

Bellasiel nodded but Kiara felt her gaze on her as she moved toward Sal, the instructor. She smiled and nodded at him, noting the tattoos on his arms that reminded her so much of Caedmon. She suddenly wondered at the chances of two ex-Army recruits being in the Refuge.

Kiara ended up staying in the training room for over an hour as Bellasiel conveniently decided to stay and observe the training. When the Elder finally disappeared, Kiara immediately made her excuses to Sal and hurried back to Teague's quarters.

She wasn't even at the door when she heard the yelling. Without hesitating, Kiara pushed the door open to find Teague holding Deanna against the wall, his hands tight around her neck, silver sparks exploding from his fingers.

The girl's color was blue and Kiara couldn't tell if she was alive or not.

"Teague!" she screamed, "Put her down."

Teague turned to Kiara his eyes wild. Then he let go of the girl and flung her across the room. As her body hit the floor with a sickening thump, Kiara stared at him.

"What have you done?" she whispered, bending to check Deanna's pulse but knowing that she'd find nothing.

Teague's eyes were wild as they scanned the room.

The door flew open and Bellasiel entered. She froze when she saw the dead girl at Kiara's feet.

"You!" Teague yelled and ran at Bellasiel his hands outstretched and silver light flashing from them. Bellasiel screamed and then was caught in the energy force.

Kiara watched in horror as he continued to advance on Bellasiel, the Elder's feet lifted from the floor until she was wholly suspended in the air. Kiara had seen this before when Mina was attacked but it wasn't the *Draíodóir* attacking that time. It had been Teague saving Mina from a Hunter. But his intentions this time were clearly to do harm!

"Teague!" Kiara called but he ignored her.

Without thinking, Kiara launched herself at Teague knocking him off his feet. He fell beneath her and hit his head on the hard floor with a sickening crunch. His eyes closed and he lost consciousness.

She should never have left Teague. Something had happened and now it seemed as if he was completely out of control.

CHAPTER FOURTEEN

It was ten days after Mina and Arion had left before Thia and Meldiron could even consider moving Xyrisse. Thia was especially happy with the healing of the Hunter girl's burns. She noticed that while Xyrisse's skin was more fragile than her own skin, it also seemed to heal faster.

To her dismay, Thia had not been able to find Teague in her dreamwalks although she looked for him almost nightly. She couldn't help thinking the worse. Since their last dreamwalk, which had ended in that huge fight, he seemed to have just disappeared completely and every additional day they stayed on the coast escalated her concern for him.

"You are worried," Xyrisse observed in her soft hissing voice as Thia reapplied her dressings.

Thia nodded silently, blinking back tears.

"Do you wish to speak of your worries?" Xyrisse queried her strange red eyes focused on Thia's face.

Thia sighed. "I don't think it will help to talk of it," she admitted sadly.

Xyrisse nodded. "It might not help the situation but you may find a bit of relief for your worries to verbalize them."

Thia looked at the girl in front of her and smiled sadly.

"Can I venture to guess your concerns center around a boy?" she asked. Thia nodded slightly, noticing how Xyrisse's strange looks did nothing to diminish her rare beauty.

"It is about a boy," Thia admitted. "A very special boy. A good friend."

She found herself telling Xyrisse about her long-standing dream relationship with Teague and how they had only just discovered one another in the waking world the previous year. She recounted the journey they'd set on with Kiara and Caedmon from the Inn and how their friendship had grown even closer on their travels. She told Xyrisse of the cave in and the People and how she had feared that Teague would be lost to her forever.

With Teague out of reach now, Thia found herself telling Xyrisse more than she'd even told her sisters. The Nasseet girl seemed to have a gift for drawing information out of people. With her sympathetic listening, Thia's worse fears bubbled to the surface and she told Xyrisse how worried she was not knowing exactly what Teague might be going through and how much she missed him.

"Even when Teague was unconscious, we were always able to connect via our dreamwalks," Thia said softly, her eyes overflowing with tears. "But now even that is gone." She looked at Xyrisse who was watching her quietly. "What if he truly is dead this time?"

Thia's voice caught as the words echoed through the small tent they were in. Now that she'd said it aloud, she knew that she'd feared that this was the case ever since she'd lost Teague in her dreams. The last time she'd seen him he'd been raving and what if he'd done something desperate?

Finally Xyrisse spoke. "What do you feel, in here?" she pointed to her chest.

Thia looked at her uncomprehending at first.

"Do you feel he has gone?" Xyrisse went on.

When Thia still didn't reply, Xyrisse gave a small sad smile. "When my brother was killed, I felt it immediately. Inside. A piece of the universe had been severed and lost forever. His lifeforce left this planet and dispersed and I felt it keenly inside." She paused. "Do you feel that Teague has gone?"

Thia considered that for a moment. She remembered suddenly what Celeste, her mentor Underground, had said about Teague when he was unconscious. She had said that she felt that he was still there but behind a film. Thia concentrated but she felt nothing. Still she didn't recognize that Teague's energy had dispersed, like Xyrisse said that she would have if such a thing had happened.

Finally Thia shook her head. "I haven't sensed his leaving," she admitted quietly. "But I can't be certain that he is still alive either."

Xyrisse inclined her head. "I think you must believe that he still lives. And you will find him again." She slowly sat up. "It seems that we must move on soon. You've already sacrificed too much to spare my life. We should leave tomorrow."

Thia's heart leapt but she looked at Xyrisse's wounds. She was doubtful that the girl was well enough to travel.

"I will be fine," Xyrisse insisted as if reading her mind. "We will go." And her hissing tone was firm. Thia could tell that the Hunter girl was accustomed to having people do as she said. It appeared she would not entertain any arguments.

An idyll thought flitted through Thia's mind. She had a sudden suspicion that Xyrisse was accustomed to holding a position of power. Shaking her head slightly, Thia discounted it as ridiculous. After all, the Nasseet would hardly let one of their most powerful leaders leave the country simply because she refused to work as a Hunter. The idea was absurd and Thia put it down to the stress of the last few weeks causing her to have fantastic thoughts. Pushing her silly speculations aside, Thia went in search of Meldiron.

#

They were amazingly efficient in packing up camp the next morning. Thia was surprised when Meldiron agreed to leave the camp. He'd been extremely concerned for Xyrisse's wellbeing and Thia had often caught the two of them having quiet talks late into the night. But Meldiron didn't even blink when Xyrisse announced that it was time for them to resume their journey.

They had decided that Xyrisse would ride with Meldiron on his horse since Thia was a weak rider at the best of times and not confident carrying a passenger on her mount. Despite her distaste for riding, Thia admitted that she was relieved to finally be on the road moving toward Teague.

It was on their third day eastward that they stumbled upon the remains of Arion and Mina's camp. It was Xyrisse who sense that something was not quite right. In fact, Thia was certain they would have ridden right past the camp if Xyrisse had not been with them.

She hissed suddenly from her place in front of Meldiron on his mount. "Stop the horses," she commanded in that regal tone again and immediately teleported off the mount. Meldiron's horse reared up in fear but the crown prince kept a tight rein on him and held the animal under control. Thia looked at Meldiron in confusion. Where had Xyrisse disappeared to? But they had no time to discuss the situation as the next moment Xyrisse was calling to them from the forest at the side of the road. Meldiron exchanged another look with Thia and then they led their horses into a clearing. Scattered throughout the clearing were three bodies. All of them were Hunters.

Thia looked at Meldiron in alarm. He strode over to the first body and crouched down to examine it. "This is Arion's work," he said as he rose, his tone confident.

Xyrisse spoke. "They were obviously on your sister's trail," she shook her head. "Three in one place. I'm sorry to say it but I fear that it is highly unlikely your friends will be successful in their journey to the Eastern mountains with this many Hunters after them."

Meldiron shook his head. "I don't think Arion would be that foolish. He knew what he was up against." He looked around the clearly. "He wouldn't have put Minathrial at risk if he could avoid it."

"He was injured in this fight," Xyrisse said suddenly.

Meldiron looked concerned. "Are you certain?" he asked.

She nodded grimly as she held up the dagger that was on the ground and sniffed it. "This is a Hunter weapon. It has Elder blood on it."

Thia looked closely at the curved blade and saw the dried blood.

"How do we know it's not Mina's blood?" Thia asked in fear. "She is Elder as well."

But Xyrisse dismissed her fear immediately. "The blood is from a male," she said with certainty.

Thia didn't want to ask how the Hunter girl knew that.

"So Arion is injured and we know Hunters are on their trail," Thia said in despair, fear for Mina causing her chest to ache. Her sister had been through so much in the last year. Her recovery from the Hunter attack had been long and arduous but Mina had emerged from that ordeal just as bubbly and enthusiastic as ever. But she had never spoken of the attack, not even to her sisters. The trauma of that event still dwelled in Mina, Thia was certain of it.

Thia looked around the clearing and wondered how her sister would have reacted to this attack. Even if Mina was somehow well physically there was no saying what her mental state might be. "What chance do they have of escape?"

Suddenly Meldiron smiled.

"What?" she asked wondering what he possibly could have to look happy about.

"Arion wouldn't continue East. He would know the odds would be stacked against them making it to the Refuge before the Hunters caught up to them."

"Then where could they have gone?" Thia asked.

Meldiron turned to the Hunter girl. "Xyrisse, you told us about the trouble Hunters have in big cities."

She nodded. "Yes, they can't pinpoint the energy from a Marked One, or even from one like Mina who has been attacked," she acknowledged quietly.

Meldiron grinned. "Then that's where Arion will have taken Minathrial. To the nearest city." He paused and beamed at Thia.

She looked at him uncomprehendingly.

"Thia, they are in Bermgarten. I'm certain of it!"

Finding Refuge

CHAPTER FIFTEEN

When Mina and Arion arrived in the large Eastern city of Bermgarten two days later, he led them deep into the heart of the city. He wasn't taking any chances on finding lodgings on the outskirts. Clearly he felt that the more hustle and bustle the safer they would be from the Hunters.

When he finally located the busy inn at the heart of the city, which was run by Helpers, Arion was able to secure them side-by-side rooms on the third floor. Even though he told Mina that they would be safe from the Hunters in Bermgarten, it quickly became apparent that he didn't want Mina exploring the city on her own. She wrinkled her nose in frustration; she was keen to see this strange new place. Finally, after a few days of being confined to the inn, Mina told him he could either accompany her or back off. To her dismay, he chose to go with her, which meant that she had to explore on his schedule. But there was some trade off. He had to go to the places *she* wanted to see! And in Bermgarten that was art.

Mina delighted in Bermgarten as much as she had in Sailsburg. She felt that, despite the attempts on her life during the journey, she was finally fulfilling her dream of seeing the world. And since they'd arrived in Bermgarten, she'd seen almost every sight that was available.

They'd been in the city five days when Mina found herself once again in the hallway outside Arion's room waiting. It seemed that all she ever did was wait for the Elder. Annoyance prickled at her senses. He'd promised, albeit reluctantly, that they could go to the Bermgarten Art Exhibit, which she'd been told about by an artist she'd met at the street market the day before, much to Arion's disapproval. He didn't like her speaking to anyone in the city. By his surly mood the previous evening, Mina could tell that he didn't truly want to attend. She didn't see why she couldn't just go to the museum on her own. The artist she'd befriended had told her that it was one of the most stunning art galleries in all of the Five Corners and boasted a collection that was both unique and eclectic. The only complication was that it opened at 9 in the morning and only let in

forty patrons a day. The artist had told her that most days there was a line
up and many people were turned away.

Mina had been determined to be first in line and she'd told Arion
that they would have to leave early. Despite his early rising on the trip to
Bermgarten, since being in the city, Mina had noticed that the dark-haired
Elder preferred to sleep for most of the morning. When she told him how
early they would have to leave, he hadn't looked excited by the idea but he
had agreed to go. And now she'd been waiting for him in her room for the
last hour and he'd yet to make an appearance. Looking at the level of the
sun out the window, Mina could tell that her chances of being admitted to
the gallery were diminishing with every second. Finally she'd decided to
wait no longer and stomped into the hallway.

She paused outside Arion's door and listened. A twinge of guilt
pricked at her. Was it really fair to wake him up so early? Absolutely, she
told herself firmly. After all he had been the one to insist that she not
explore the city without him. If he was going to be so stubborn then he had
to make some sacrifices on his sleep. Besides he could have gone to bed
early. She *had* told him they were leaving early!

"Arion! Are you ready yet?" Mina called through the door after
she finished pounding on it. She listened for a few minutes and pounded on
the door again. Still no answer.

Arion seemed determined to sleep in and make her miss the one
exhibit she had been dying to see. Shaking her head in frustration, Mina
made a quick decision. She could either leave on her own or wait for him
and surely miss her chance. It was no contest.

Mina raced down the hallway excitement pounding in her chest.
She was actually going to explore the city on her own! Grinning she
stepped into the city street, a spring in her step. The sun was out and there
were people everywhere on the street. She loved the hustle and bustle of
the street vendors and women running through the streets on their errands.

And the architecture in this city was so unique. Houses were built
incredibly high. Mina looked up at them as she wandered below,
fascinated by their height.

Mina was so excited to be exploring on her own that she didn't
really notice where she was going. That was until she realized that she had
no idea which direction the art gallery was located in. She looked up and
saw that she'd wandered into an unfamiliar part of the city. Looking back
over her shoulder, she felt a beat of alarm when she realized that she
couldn't see any familiar landmarks behind her either. Instead the street

was lined with warehouses and boarded up shops. All at once, Mina noticed the other people on the street. Rough around the edges, men with hard eyes and gruff words. There were children begging on the corners and she saw more than one pitiful creature collapsed in a doorway, sleeping or otherwise unconscious.

Cursing her impatience and lack of attention, Mina stopped suddenly in the street trying to find her bearings. A delivery boy crashed roughly into her back. "Watch it, Miss. Whatcha doin'?"

"Sorry," Mina murmured but the boy was gone. She continued her frontward motion and frowned. How could she have so quickly wandered off course? Why hadn't she paid better attention to the location of the inn when she went out with Arion? She'd spent most of her time in the city so far too excited to pay any attention to her surroundings. Stupid, stupid, stupid!

Mina held up her head and walked with purpose even though her heart was beginning to pound. She'd carelessly wandered into a rough part of the city and she had no idea where she was going. She thought she was a world traveler but since leaving the Inn back home, she'd not once ventured out on her own to explore. She'd always had Meldiron or Thia or Arion with her. And now, the one time she did take off by herself, she got lost and could potentially be in a dangerous position.

Almost as if her frantic thoughts had conjured them up, out of the corner of her eye Mina saw a group of five or six rough-looking young men pointing in her direction. Pretending not to notice them, she picked up her pace.

Her heart sank as she glimpsed the ruffians falling into step ten paces behind her. Mina turned at the next road and they followed. She quickened her pace. As long as she looked like she was expected somewhere, surely she would be safe, she reasoned. After all this was broad daylight. Surely, they wouldn't dare to approach her in the middle of the morning. But, looking ahead, she was dismayed to see that the road she'd stepped onto looked even more deserted than the others.

Knowing it was the wrong thing to do but unable to stop herself she broke into a run. She heard a yell from the pack following her and she knew she'd made another fatal mistake. Choking back a sob, Mina desperately turned down the next opening in the street to find herself in a deserted alley and it ended in a sturdy brick wall. There was no exit.

Trembling she turned around to face her pursuers. They were exchanging crude remarks and grins.

Mina took a deep breath and decided to try to reason with them. After all she had nothing they could possibly want.

"Ooops, I must have taken a wrong turn," she said less confidently than she'd hoped, her voice coming out high and squeaky. "Excuse me, gentlemen." She took a step in their direction hoping against hope they would step aside and make way for her.

They looked at her as if she'd lost her mind.

"Not so fast, chickie, pretty little thing like you," said the tall, broad one who seemed to be their leader. His long hair hung in his face in greasy strings and Mina felt a shiver of repulsion streak through her. She took one more tentative step hoping to duck past them and then the big one grabbed her arms.

"We'll have some fun with this one, eh boys?" He pulled her flush against his body, his foul breathe making her choke.

"Let me go!" she sobbed, fear squeezing her chest.

"I don't think so," he said grabbing her face with a callused hand. "You're a fine beauty," he breathed his hot eyes lighting up in a way that made Mina's stomach roll. She wondered vaguely if he would let her go if she threw up on him?

"I'll have the first turn with her, lads, then you can each have a turn." He groped the neckline of her dress and terror streaked through her. Mina didn't want to imagine what he planned to do to her. Spittle dripped from his mouth as his eyes dropped to her cleavage.

Mina screamed at the top of her lungs and the ruffian swore foully before he cuffed her on the side of the head making her ears ring.

"Stop that," he growled.

Before he could say anymore, he was flying against the side of the alley. His head hit the wall so hard it gave a resounding crack and he crumbled to the ground. The others surged forward and then Mina saw Arion, his dagger flashing dangerously in the dim light. Relief coursed through her followed by panic as she realized he was outnumbered and his shoulder was not yet healed. But Arion moved like lightening. This encounter was even more lethal than his face off with the Hunters in the clearing. Three more of the gang fell and the rest scattered running for their lives. Mina vaguely noted that it was probably the wisest choice on their part. Arion certainly looked capable of murder.

Mina was rooted to the ground trembling as she looked over at the body of her attacker. He was obviously dead, a pool of dark blood under his head. She flinched when Arion touched her shoulder.

"Princess. Look at me." Mina dragged her eyes away from the crumbled figure and looked unseeingly in Arion's direction. Small sobs were escaping her lips. Arion reached out and pulled her neckline into place, averting his eyes as he did so. Then Mina's legs gave out as the full horror of what had almost happened occurred to her.

Arion swept her up into his arms. Whispering reassurances in the Elder language until they washed over her in a steady tide, he carried her through the streets back to their lodgings.

When they returned to the inn, Arion tucked her into her bed and ordered some tea delivered to her room. Despite the warm blankets, Mina couldn't stop shivering. Arion sat on the edge of her bed and forced her to sip the hot beverage, which he'd prepared with generous amounts of honey and milk.

When she calmed down at last and reluctantly forced herself to meet his eyes, she was gratified to see no judgment or censor in the pale green depths. Instead his eyes were filled with concern and something deeper that she couldn't identify.

"I'm sorry," she whispered and looked down at her hands, resting on the blanket.

Arion didn't answer for a moment. At last he said, "Why, Princess?" When she looked up at him he went on. "Why would you do something so foolish?"

She swallowed and felt her cheeks heat as she remembered how determined she'd been to find her own way through the city. It seemed silly now.

"I wasn't thinking. You weren't answering your door and I wanted to go to the art exhibit." Mina forced herself not to cringe as she heard how childish her words sounded.

Arion raised his brows. "You weren't anywhere near that part of the city."

She nodded dropping her gaze again. "I don't know my way around very well," she admitted, shamefully. Then added defensively. "You haven't exactly encouraged me to navigate on my own through Bermgarten."

"Do you realize how much danger you were in?" he asked gravely, his tone neutral.

Mina remembered the foul stench of her attacker's breath, his rough fingers groping into her dress. A sob escaped her lips again and she nodded as hot tears spilled onto her cheeks.

Biting out a curse in Elder language, Arion suddenly pulled her into his arms and she went willingly. His strong hands drew comforting circles on her back as he murmured Elder words of reassurance in her ear. Mina was vaguely aware that she could easily understand what he was saying.

Eventually her sobs abated and she became aware of Arion's heart beating steadily beneath her ear. She should pull away but she didn't want to. It felt … nice.

He continued to hold her. "Do you know how important you are?" he asked after a few more minutes.

Mina looked up at him. He kept insisting how vital she was but Mina didn't really understand because he never explained it to her.

"To the Elder people?" she asked softly.

Arion looked down at her, his face unreadable. "To the Elder people, yes." His gaze dropped to her lips and he looked like he would say more but then suddenly he pulled away and stood.

Mina watched at him in confusion, trying not to feel hurt at his abrupt departure. Arion was a complex character.

She looked away and leaned back into the headboard behind her. To her horror tears filled her eyes again. And then Arion was kneeling by the bed.

"Don't cry." The pain in his voice was raw. "When I found you in that alley today," he closed his eyes to the memory. "Mina, I lost control. If anything had happened to you …"

She stared at him in surprise, hardly believing that he called her by her nickname.

"I'm sorry." She reached up and cupped his cheek until he opened his eyes. "I was not hurt." It was true. The ruffians had scared her but she was unharmed.

He shook his head. "But you could have been. And it is my responsibility to ensure your safety."

Mina felt as if he had slapped her with the word responsibility. Clearly she was just a burden to him.

"But I wasn't hurt," she said coldly.

He watched her for a few silent moments then seemed to come to a decision. He stood and held out his hand to her.

She looked at it questioningly.

"I think it's time you learned to fend for yourself."

Mina narrowed her eyes, wondering what he meant.

"Princess, you need to commence your training. Training that should have been done years ago."

Mina looked at Arion's strong hand extended toward her. Training? She couldn't begin to understand what he meant but a tingle of excitement started to course through her.

And then, suddenly feeling almost as if she were discovering her destiny, Mina put her hand in Arion's ready to face her future head on.

CHAPTER SIXTEEN

"I can't believe that you haven't had any kind of defensive training at all. If you'd been in Séreméla, the training would have been part of your education. I'm surprised Meldiron didn't start you on it while you were with the Elders."

Mina shrugged as she followed him down the stairs. Arion had given her a pair of pale green tight fitting trousers and a loose tunic to wear. He was wearing similar clothes. How he had come to have such items in precisely her size Mina couldn't say.

"I was still recovering while I was in Séreméla," she reminded him, "I don't think physical training would have been possible then."

Arion nodded. "Well, it needs to start now. There are just too many possible dangers that you could run into and if something happened to me, you'd be completely defenseless."

Mina had to admit that he was right. But they were trying to keep a low profile while in Bermgarten. "Won't it draw attention if we start sparring in the stable yard?"

Arion laughed and Mina couldn't help noticing how the light danced in his pale eyes when he did so. For a moment she was distracted by just how attractive he was but then she noticed that he didn't stop laughing at her.

"What is so funny?"

He sobered at her words. "Well, sparring in the stable yard," here a chuckle escaped. Mina scowled at him. "I'm sorry. But that kind of training would draw attention, yes. Is that how they did it at the Inn?" he teased. "It is different in other parts of the Five Corners."

Mina shook her head in confusion. Kiara had always trained in the stableyard. She didn't understand why it was so amusing to Arion.

He held out his hand. "Come on, I'll show you."

Mina put her hand in his and let him pull her toward the street. He released her as soon as they were on their way but Mina could still feel the warmth from his brief touch.

"Where are we going?" she asked as he led her into the busy street. She tried to ignore how her hand still tingled from his touch.

"You'll see," he told her vaguely.

Arion led her through the winding streets of Bermgarten as if it were his hometown. She was continually amazed at how easily he'd oriented himself to the new city.

Finally he stopped in front of a building that was atypical for Bermgarten. The city was so condensed that most buildings were tall, narrow stone structures with their entrances opening to the street. But the building Arion was standing in front of now had a small gate that opened to a garden path and led to a small one storied building that was made entirely of wood and glass.

He turned and smiled at her as he opened the door. Mina followed him inside and then gasped. The inside of the building was a large open room that was filled with people sparring.

"What is this?" Mina asked softly.

"A training house," Arion explained.

Mina looked around the room. There were Bermgartians from all walks of life in various forms of combat. She saw an elderly woman with white hair flip a young man almost as tall as Arion onto the mat. Across the room a small girl was sparring with a larger boy, he seemed to be instructing her.

Mina looked at Arion. "So we won't draw attention?"

"Not in Bermgarten."

#

Arion and Mina began training for several hours every morning. Mina quickly grew to love the training house and the routine and she knew she was getting better at defending herself. Arion had explained that in Bermgarten it was important for everyone to be able to defend themselves as raiders from the mountains were common. Early on in the city's history, the training houses had been constructed and all citizens were encouraged to use them.

Mina noticed that the training house they went to was almost always full. Clearly the citizens of Bermgarten took their training seriously.

A few weeks into their new routine, they were walking home a different route from the training house. Mina was once again utterly lost.

"We are going to need to teach you how to navigate, Mina," Arion observed as she peered hopelessly around the city streets, completely lost yet again. She smiled at his use of her nickname. Arion hadn't called her Princess or Minathrial in days now. She liked the familiarity and he seemed to have adjusted to the informality.

"Do you think that's possible?" she asked with a laugh.

"Anything is possible," Arion told her confidently.

After that they began to wander the city streets at all times of the day and night. Arion would lead her along a new route and force her to find their way back. At first, Mina couldn't do it. She would just get them more and more lost. But then Arion taught her the trick of noting landmarks that would help her to remember the path back to the inn. In the beginning Mina would get turned around but then Arion reminded her that she needed to turn opposite from the turns they took on the way out. Soon she had become so good at navigating that Arion would blindfold her on the way out and have her lead them back.

One night when he removed the blindfold, Mina saw they were in an unfamiliar part of the city. She looked around but didn't recognize anything. She scanned the skyline for familiar buildings but everything was new. Arion had taught her to avoid wandering aimlessly from the beginning.

Mina wrinkled her nose at a loss for what to do. "Okay, Arion, you got me this time. I have no idea which was to go."

He smiled at her. "Progress! At least you aren't going off on a wild foray through the streets at night. You are learning, Mina!"

Mina nodded but then frowned. "But what do I do if I find myself in this kind of dilemma? I can't stand on the street forever."

Arion came and stood behind her. Mina swallowed trying to ignore the close proximity of him. Despite the fact that their relationship stayed professional, Mina couldn't deny that Arion had an affect on her. She noticed that he appeared immune to her presence and she tried to attain the same level of indifference as he had. But she feared that she wasn't as successful as he. He grasped her shoulders and pointed to the sky. "You need to learn to read the stars."

Mina turned to look at him, suddenly realizing how close they were. Her heart began to pound. Arion stepped back.

Wanting to cut the sudden tension, Mina focused on his words and asked weakly, "Read the stars?"

Arion nodded. "The night sky doesn't change. It can guide you when you are lost."

Mina looked back up at the stars intrigued. "How?" she asked.

"I will teach you."

\#

Once Mina had learned to find her way through the city, Arion relaxed a bit about her wandering on her own. To be honest, Mina thought he was a bit relieved. She knew he only went to the art exhibits because he was worried something would happen to her. He had no interest in them and didn't try to hide his boredom. It was a sign of her progress when he first let her go alone. They came to an agreement that she could explore on her own with the caveat that she would not go anywhere new without Arion. The first time she went to a new place, Arion would accompany her. After he was satisfied it was safe, she could go by herself. He often would just accompany her for the first quarter of an hour and then he would go his own way once he was satisfied that there was no threat to her. Where he went, she didn't know but Mina was happy to have some independence again. And to be honest, she thought Arion probably enjoyed his time away from her as well.

But it was because of his one stipulation that Mina found herself dragging Arion out in the early hours one day.

"It looks like a shop of novelties," Mina told him, her excitement bubbling over. She'd found the shop on her way home from the Bermgarten Library the previous day. She'd been tempted to go inside but she knew Arion would not approve of that.

"Novelties?" he asked, confusion tingeing his words.

"Well, you know, odds and ends and other stuff. I thought I saw a painting like the one in the gallery I went to last week hidden behind some old junk. But it was too hard to tell looking through the window. I want to go in." Arion rolled his eyes. "If you don't want to come with me I'll go on my own," Mina offered innocently, knowing there was no way he would agree to that.

"Absolutely not," he said firmly as he stood up and followed her out of the inn.

Mina smiled to herself. She knew he'd never approve of her going on her own and if she was honest she'd admit that she wanted to get his feedback on the variety of things she saw in the shop. She thought she'd caught a glimpse of some scripts with the Elder language on them but it was too dusty on the outer windows to tell for sure.

They stepped inside the dingy store and the greasy proprietor came forward. "Welcome," he said in a slippery tone, his eyes lingered for a bit too long on Mina's hair. Arion suddenly slipped his arm around her.

"What did you want to look at, love?" he asked her in a doting tone. Mina was so shocked by his sudden playacting that she couldn't answer for a moment. She had no idea he was so gifted at acting.

She looked around the shop but the art she thought she'd seen from the street was nowhere in sight. Still there was a pile of scrolls and books scattered on a large table.

She slipped out from under Arion's arm and moved toward the table. Another table, one in the Séreméla library, that had been scattered with a similar mess came to mind painfully.

"Mina? What's wrong?" Arion whispered so the proprietor wouldn't hear him.

Mina shook her head, trying to get the image of Eöl Ar-Feiniel's lifeless body out of her head. She shifted the scrolls on the table around. They were piles of business documents long forgotten, there was a book on Bermgarten's history that looked interesting and then a scroll in ancient Elder script caught her attention. She unrolled it and gasped. The words of the Prophecy jumped off the page at her.

"Oh that just arrived. It is genuine Elder history," the shopkeeper said quickly as he saw her interest. "Very rare. Very precious."

Arion was at Mina's side in an instant. He looked over the scroll and then shook his head dismissively.

"That's not genuine," he scoffed.

Mina stared hard at him. The scroll was very clearly at least part of the Prophecy if not a complete copy.

The slimy little man raised his eyebrows. "I assure you it is."

Arion glared at him. "Do you think you know a genuine Elder scroll better than I do?" he asked, his voice filled with distain.

The man looked uncertain, his beady eyes shifting from side to side. "It came from a good source," he insisted but his words sounded doubtful.

"Well, your source seems to have sold you a fake," Arion told him. "See this and this," he pointed to the edging of the scroll. "Not Elder at all. This scroll is worthless. You'd better not let anyone see you trying to sell a fake in Bermgarten."

The man's widened his dark eyes in fear.

"Darling, if you want the history book I'll buy it for you. There's nothing else of worth here," Arion told Mina his eyes flashing at warning at her.

Mina schooled her features trying to decipher what kind of game Arion was playing. They both knew the scroll was not a fake. What was he doing? How could he suggest they leave it there?

"Wait!" the proprietor said suddenly, "Can you take the scroll – just so it's out of here? If I dispose of it people will be suspicious."

Arion looked at it and wrinkled his nose. "What would I want with it?"

"I don't know but please – you know Elder paper is not burnable and if I throw it in the bin someone is bound to find it and trace it back to me."

Mina spoke up, "We could take it, what harm would there be in that?"

Reluctantly Arion nodded. And fifteen minutes later they walked out of the shop with what appeared to be a full copy of the Lost Prophecy.

CHAPTER SEVENTEEN

Kiara stood in the room staring at the body of Deanna after they'd taken Teague away.

"I should have seen this coming," Bellasiel said quietly behind her.

Kiara turned, startled. She hadn't realized that Bellasiel was still in the room.

"Don't blame yourself, Kiara, you couldn't have known how far the *Draíodóir* had corrupted his mind. I'm sorry the girl was killed, I know you were fond of her."

Kiara dragged her eyes away from Deanna's lifeless form and looked at Bellasiel uncomprehendingly. "You knew something like this could happen?" she asked, her voice raw with emotion, struggling to understand.

Bellasiel sighed. "Omen and I suspected something like this *might* happen. Teague has been becoming more and more violent."

Kiara thought of how Teague had reacted to Omen's presence the previous day. "Are you sure his violence is not because of what Omen is doing to his mind? Teague was terrified to be left alone with him when he came by yesterday."

Bellasiel shook her head. "Teague is delusional. You have my word that Omen only had his best interests in mind."

Kiara couldn't help wondering what Bellasiel's word was worth. Teague hadn't been violent at all before Kiara left him that morning. If anything he had been as if *he* needed protecting. And then he suddenly killed an innocent girl the moment she was summoned away. Summoned unnecessarily, she remembered. It didn't make any sense. Rage suddenly infused her. Kiara did not like anyone to make her feel like the fool and that's precisely what the Elder was doing. Did she think Kiara was stupid and couldn't see what was going on here?

"I don't believe you," Kiara stated flatly, looking Bellasiel in the eye. "Teague was fine when I left him."

Bellasiel met her eyes steadily. "I know you don't want to think that your friend did this, Kiara. That's understandable. I can have Omen come and speak to you if you want. He can explain what has happened to Teague." She paused. "Unless you have a rational explanation for why Teague would do this?"

Kiara looked down at Deanna's lifeless form on the floor. Her anger suddenly dispersed. Regret filled her as she remembered how she'd told the girl to stay with Teague. She didn't have an explanation for what had happened but she knew deep down that Omen was somehow behind it. Maybe if she could speak to the former *Draíodóir* herself she could start to figure out exactly what was going on here. She looked at Bellasiel.

"Fine. I'll speak to Omen. And I want to see Teague later."

Bellasiel nodded. "Of course, my dear. You may see Teague whenever you wish," she said soothingly, "Ah, here is Omen now."

The small weasel-like man had just arrived at the room and was looking at Deanna's body on the floor with a satisfied expression. When he realized Kiara was watching him, he cleared his features of all emotion.

Kiara didn't need any more convincing. Red filled her vision as she looked at the one responsible for all of this. Before she could think she'd flown across the room and pinned him to the wall, her forearm tight against his throat. She felt her own stab of satisfaction when she heard the gurgling noises he was making

"What did you do?" she screamed at him. "I know you're responsible for this. What have you done to Teague's mind?"

But the man didn't answer her, instead he was making gasping noises and his eyes were filled with panic as he realized he couldn't pull any oxygen into his lungs.

"I don't think he can answer your questions since you're crushing his vocal chords," Bellasiel noted drily.

The red anger clouding Kiara's mind faded abruptly and she stepped back, dropping Omen to the ground where he lay wheezing and moaning for several minutes like the coward she was convinced he was. Kiara stood over him and waited.

Finally he looked up. His earlier expression of satisfaction had been replaced with one of fear. She'd scared him. Good, he deserved to be scared.

"What did you do to Teague?" she demanded again.

He looked up at her, sadness filling his eyes. "I swear I did nothing to him," he said his tone filled with insincere sorrow.

"He was fine when I was conveniently lured away under false pretenses," Kiara pointed out.

"No, Kiara, you're wrong. Teague wasn't okay," Omen said as he weakly climbed to his feet. "He'd been growing more and more unstable over the last few weeks. He was becoming paranoid, distrusting everyone." He looked down at the dead child on the ground. "I never imagined his paranoia would elevate to this extreme." Although he was clearly trying to sound sincere Kiara could hear the falsehoods under the pretense of caring.

His words reeked of lies to Kiara.

"He didn't seem paranoid when I stayed with him all day yesterday and last night," she pointed out, sure that Omen was hiding something.

"Didn't he? Remember how he reacted when I came to the door?" Kiara reluctantly thought back to Teague's extreme reaction to Omen's visit. She'd put it down to the fact that he was feeling terrorized by Omen but could it be something else? Doubt slivered its way into her mind.

Omen staggered over to a chair and lowered himself into it. He looked up at Kiara pleadingly, "Try to understand. What the *Draíodóir* did to his mind was extreme. It isn't his fault he's acting the way he is. The *Draíodóir* recognized what Teague was from the moment they laid hands on him."

"And what precisely is Teague?" Kiara asked suspiciously, remembering Thia's story of the Underground and how they had insisted Teague was more than just a *Draíodóir*.

Omen pressed his lips together. "A Marked One and a *Draíodóir*. That makes him very powerful and useful to the *Draíodóir* brotherhood."

So Omen didn't know about the People and the fact that Teague was also a Halfling. She kept her mouth shut, waiting to see where Omen was going with this, her distrust of him still strong.

"The *Draíodóir* have woven complex ties throughout Teague's mind to keep him connected to them. They are desperate to retain control of him." He paused and seemed to be searching for words. "Try to imagine Teague's mind as a field that has been filled with hidden traps and obstacles. At every step there is the danger that a new trap will be sprung and Teague will be lost. The *Draíodóir* philosophy is that if one of their own is captured by outsiders, they would rather destroy his mind than risk having others privy to their secrets."

Kiara remembered how Thia had described the spell that Teague had fallen under in the cave. It had been based on the same philosophy. What he was saying was true but Kiara couldn't help thinking that Omen was weaving his tale with strategically placed slivers of truth amid an abundance of manipulative lies.

"Are you suggesting that Teague is under some kind of *Draíodóirian* spell?"

Omen nodded running with his story. "A terrible spell. This one is destroying Teague as you know him." He sighed. "You're right in a sense. What Teague did here was partially my own fault. You see, weeks ago I helped Teague construct a mental wall against the *Draíodóir*. We could not risk having them discover the Refuge."

Kiara tilted her head thoughtfully. She knew that Teague's mind link with the *Draíodóir* was dangerous. That was one of the reasons they'd come straight to the Refuge when they left Séreméla. They had hoped that Omen would be able to help Teague learn a way to resist the *Draíodóir* voices in his head.

"So how is what happened partially your fault?" she asked wondering where he was going with his story.

"The wall Teague constructed seemed to have worked. And I think it still is working as we've had no indication that the *Draíodóir* have discovered where we are. But what I didn't suspect was that the *Draíodóir* may have laid another trap in Teague's mind. Perhaps it has something to do with how long he's been out of contact with them. Whatever it is, I noticed that Teague started behaving irrationally about three weeks ago. And he's become steadily worse. When I arrived yesterday I was hoping to work with him to see if we could somehow override whatever spell the *Draíodóir* have left in his mind. But you turned me away," he paused, "I'm not blaming you, Kiara. You've known Teague longer than I have and it makes sense that you would take his word over my own. I admit I did come back while you were in the training rooms this morning and Teague and the little girl were playing a game. But when Teague saw me he became agitated. Seeing that I wasn't getting anywhere with him, I left. I never imagined he would harm the child." He looked down at Deanna's body sorrowfully.

Kiara stared at Omen. Her instincts told her that he wasn't telling the whole truth even if his story did make sense. Kiara couldn't shake the suspicion that Omen was a well-rehearsed liar. She made a decision.

"Teague has been under a spell like this before," she began cautiously.

His eyes flickered with interest that he quickly tried to hide.

"My sister, Thia, said he fell into a coma when he was injured Underground. The People were not able to bring him out of it and the only way she could contact him was through the dreamwalks." Kiara paused as she remembered Teague's certainty that Omen had cast a spell on him making him unable to sleep. "Did you do something to Teague hindering his ability to sleep?"

Omen looked at her steadily. "We were working on a sleep solution. The lack of sleep obviously didn't help his paranoia. But I couldn't break that spell."

Kiara narrowed her eyes. It was clear that Omen was going to blame everything on a *Draíodóirian* spell. Her gut told her to tread carefully with the information she gave to this man.

"How did Teague recovered from the other spell?" Omen asked casually.

The question was too casual, Kiara sensed. If he thought he was a practiced liar, then he was about to meet his match. She shrugged. "We don't know. He suddenly woke when they arrived above ground," Kiara lied. There was no way she was going to tell this man about her sister's seizures and energy work.

She saw confusion flash across Omen's face followed by disappointment. She was convinced he was weaving a tale, at least part of the time. Kiara turned to Bellasiel who was instructing the two workers who'd come to take Deanna's body. Kiara watched as they lifted the remains of the little girl and felt another pang of guilt. She should have taken care of her. Honestly, she'd owed that much to her and instead she'd only hastened her death. Kiara blinked back sudden tears as she thought of the hard life little Deanna had led. The poor girl had witnessed more violence in her short life than anyone should have to. Kiara had hoped to give her a better life. She'd failed her. Now, as she watched them leave with Deanna's body, she could only ask herself if the little girl wouldn't have been better off left with her mother in the first place?

She forced her attention to the Elder. She had to focus on Teague now.

"Bellasiel, where did they take Teague?"

Bellasiel turned her to Kiara, her expression grim. "They took him to the lower levels. Kiara, are you sure you want to see him? You do understand that we have to restrain him to protect the other children who are here."

The fact that Bellasiel was trying to talk her out of seeing Teague just made her desire to see him even stronger.

"Take me to him," she said grimly.

#

Kiara shouldn't have been surprised to find the lower levels were actually more akin to dungeons. The walls were rock and it was dark and damp and dingy. As she moved lower into the mines she couldn't help feeling the oppression of miles of rock and earth above her. She was sure this was not going to be good for Teague in his current state of mind and when she found him it was even worse she had imagined.

The guards who had brought Teague to the lower levels had chained him to the far wall. Kiara was surprised to see that they had already fashioned cells down here. Once again she couldn't help wondering how long the Refuge had been planned before they came here. Prison cells such as these were not built in mere hours. And why had they even thought to make prison cells part of the Refuge, she wondered, a shiver running down her spine.

Kiara was horrified to find Teague unconscious and hanging by his arms from the chains that were around his wrists. A sob caught in her throat when she saw him.

"Teague!" she called, hoping to wake him. Teague groaned slightly moving his head and Kiara saw fresh bruises and a cut on his lip. Clearly the guards had done more than just bring him down to the dungeons. They had obviously given him a good beating before they chained him up. No doubt if questioned they would say that he had resisted them.

Kiara felt sick to her stomach. She wondered what Caedmon would do when he discovered what had happened to his brother. She could only imagine how furious he would be. And she was supposed to look after Teague while he was gone. She'd done a horrible job of that, hadn't she? Obviously she wasn't cut out to be the caretaker of anyone. Both Deanna and Teague were proof of that.

After it became clear that Teague was not going to respond to her calls, Kiara left the dungeons and began climbing upward. There was nothing she could do for Teague while he was unconscious. When would Caedmon return? What was the urgent business he needed to attend to?

Where had he gone? Had he known how sick Teague really was? And was there any way for her to contact him?

Kiara wondered what she should do. She wasn't sure whom she could trust anymore. For now she would have to keep her worries and speculations about Teague to herself.

She just hoped Caedmon would return soon.

#

Unfortunately, it was another three days before Caedmon returned to the Refuge. During that time, Kiara had stayed with Teague as much as possible but he was unconscious most of the time. She didn't know if it was due to the beating he'd suffered or shock from what he'd done. When he did open his eyes, he stared unseeingly across the room, moaning and sobbing. Clearly Teague knew what he had done to Deanna and he was distraught with grief. As much as she tried to calm him down it was to no avail. Finally she left him, sensing that her presence only agitated him more.

Kiara was outside in the same spot where they'd had their last discussion, when she saw Caedmon coming out up the path to the Refuge. She took a deep breath. Inside joy at seeing him again was warring with dread of having to tell him what had happened in his absence.

She stood to meet him, her eyes drawn to his broad, strong frame. Kiara wanted nothing more than to sink into his embrace but she didn't think he'd want her anywhere near him when he learned of what she'd let happen.

"Caedmon," she called, deciding to get it over with. And he quickened his pace reaching to pull her into his arms when he saw who was calling him. He gave her a kiss and laughed. But when Kiara remained stiff in his arms and he pulled back slightly to look down at her face. He let her go immediately when he saw her grim expression. "What's wrong?"

There was no point in beating around the bush. "It's Teague," she admitted.

All trace of humor and happiness was erased from Caedmon's face. "What happened?" he asked roughly.

Kiara took a deep breath it wasn't going to be easy telling Caedmon what had happened but she learned a long time ago it was better just to give the full story without trying to gloss over anything, She sat Caedmon down on a rock far enough away from the entrance to the Refuge that no one would overhear what she had to say. And she told him everything that had happened from the moment he left until Teague had been chained up.

"They beat him, Caedmon," she admitted. "He's only just regained consciousness in the last few hours but he doesn't know who I am. He's distraught most of the time. I think he realizes what he did and, you know Teague, it's destroying him. But I'm certain it was *not* his fault."

Kiara had had more time to analyze what had happened in the last few days and it just didn't make sense that Teague would suddenly turn on Deanna. Ugly thoughts were starting to eat at Kiara's mind as she remembered Bellasiel insisting that she stay in the training room that morning and Omen's attempt to see Teague the day before. In addition, she remembered Bellasiel's annoyance over the presence of Deanna at the Refuge. Kiara was almost completely convinced that the two of them had devised a plan to have Teague kill the girl. And that meant they would somehow have control over him now. She didn't know how they did it but the more she thought about it, the more it made sense to her.

She tried to share her suspicions with Caedmon but she didn't think she was being very clear as tears choked her words.

Caedmon listened to the whole story in silence but the muscles in his shoulders were bunching and his face was darker when she was done.

"Perhaps when he sees you he will come around," Kiara said softly tentatively putting her hand on Caedmon's large arm.

He stood abruptly and stormed into the Refuge. The explosion of movement made Kiara jump before she hurried after him. She knew better than to try to talk Caedmon when he was in this mood.

She wanted Caedmon's opinion about her suspicions of Bellasiel and Omen but she knew his first concern would be finding his brother and seeing how badly he was injured. She also knew that Caedmon did not believe that Teague had lost his mind. She was sure that he wouldn't let himself believe that.

She remembered how Teague had been certain that Bellasiel was building her own army of Marked children. Kiara felt a shiver run down her spine as she wondered if they'd been manipulated from the very beginning even before they left Séreméla. They had all believed that Bellasiel was on their side but what if she was a different kind of enemy. She remembered how Meldiron had warned them not to trust anyone. But Meldiron had told them they could trust Bellasiel. Could it be that the Elder prince was wrong when it came to the old healer? Maybe he was correct with his first warning not to trust anyone who was not Marked.

And now they not only had the responsibility of looking after Teague but also of protecting the Marked children they brought to the Refuge.

Over the last few days, Kiara had begun to notice how Bellasiel treated the young children almost as if they were objects. She wondered if Bellasiel saw them as just that: a means to achieve her ends. What if Bellasiel was intent on starting some kind of war against enemies that Kiara and the others didn't even know were against them? But who might those enemies be?

Bellasiel had left Kiara largely alone since the episode with Teague and Deanna. In fact she hadn't seen Bellasiel in several days now. She felt certain as she followed Caedmon into the depths of the mine that he would not lie as low as she had when he came to dealing with the Elder.

"Where to now?" Caedmon asked as he reached the fork in the road that led either to the training grounds or deeper into the mines.

"Here I'll show you," Kiara said stepping ahead of him.

They went lower into the mines and she could see Caedmon's jaw harden as he noticed the moisture on the walls and the dark dank smell that came from the depths. As a former member of the army, Kiara was certain that Caedmon would be familiar with such places. It was a miserable place to put someone. The perfect location for dungeons, perhaps, but Teague did not belong in the dungeon, she was sure of it.

Kiara slowed as she got closer to the cells. She'd been down to visit Teague earlier that morning and he'd been unconscious again. He'd looked worse than when they had first taken him to the dungeons, the bruises on his face blossoming into ugly black and yellow marks. She didn't know how Caedmon would react when he saw his brother. She'd tried to warn him that Teague was in bad shape.

Caedmon pushed passed her as she halted in the entrance to the dungeons. He strode purposefully toward his brother's cell.

"Teague," he called gruffly.

Teague let out a soft moan at the sound of his brother's voice.

Caedmon tried to open the cell and found that it was locked. He growled in frustration.

"Who has the keys to the cell?" he demanded, his voice dangerously quiet, more dangerous than if he had bellowed.

Kiara shook her head. She didn't know. "Bellasiel will know who has the keys," she told him. She was frightened by the rage she saw in his eyes.

Kiara remembered how ruthlessly Caedmon had killed enemies in the past. She was glad that she was not Bellasiel at the moment.

Caedmon strode past her returning to the upper levels with his speed that was inhuman. Kiara found herself running to try to keep up with him. But she soon gave up and contented herself with meeting him at Bellasiel's office. He had no trouble locating Bellasiel in her office and he burst through her doors without knocking.

"You have some explaining to do," he growled. "Why is my brother locked up and where are the keys to the dungeons?"

Bellasiel merely looked up from some papers almost as if she'd been expecting Caedmon. Kiara was surprised at how unruffled she appeared by Caedmon's angry words.

"Your brother killed an innocent child," Bellasiel told him sternly. "He is locked up for everyone's safety especially that of the Marked children. We can't take any chances that he might attack again."

Caedmon was livid. "I do not believe that my brother would kill a child. There had to be extenuating circumstances."

"Ask Kiara - she was there unlike you. I could ask where you disappeared to, Caedmon. Or if your expedition was successful but perhaps that is for another time."

Kiara looked at Caedmon wondering what Bellasiel was talking about. Did the Elder know where he had gone? Caedmon hadn't even told her – how had Bellasiel discovered his destination? Caedmon remained silent, face passive but his dark eyes glinting dangerously.

Bellasiel remained unruffled. "Kiara saw what your brother did. He is a danger to everyone around him. We will be lucky if Omen is able to make it so that the *Draíodóir* don't track us here now, thanks to your brother."

Kiara saw Caedmon's face darken with rage. She saw him clenching his hands and knew that he was fighting for control over himself. Bellasiel was making him very angry. Kiara wondered if she was purposely provoking him. The Elder seemed to want to push him.

Caedmon stared at Bellasiel. "Even if he is as dangerous as you say he is, you have him chained to a wall. There is no need to lock his cell as well. Unless you're worried others will get to him. Why is the cell locked?"

Bellasiel did not answer him.

"I want the keys to his cell. If anyone needs to get to Teague they're going to have to go through me."

Bellasiel looked up and for a moment Kiara thought she might argue with him. But then Caedmon went on, "Your guards have clearly been taking turns beating the life out of my brother. Is there a reason that you want to beat him down? What is it that Omen is planning to do to him? Do you think I'm stupid? I know the tactics of those who torture their prisoners. I was in the Army or are you forgetting? It is obvious to me that Omen wants my brother weakened before he works on his mind."

Bellasiel answered angrily and Kiara was surprised when she didn't deny it, "Do you blame him? Look at the damage he did to that girl. He could easily do the same to Omen."

"Would he have more reason to do the same to Omen?" Kiara couldn't help asking. Bellasiel shifted her attention to her.

"I've been thinking about what happened to Teague," Kiara explained. "It's kind of convenient that he killed Deanna, isn't it? After all you wanted to get rid of the girl right from the second you realize she wasn't Marked. I can't help wondering if you had Teague do your dirty work for you."

Bellasiel's eyes narrowed. Kiara regretted her words almost instantly. She had not meant to share her suspicions with Bellasiel. She hadn't even shared them with Caedmon yet. Now because of her big mouth, the Elder knew that she didn't trust her.

Caedmon spoke. "Bellasiel, give me the keys to my brother's cell. If you don't give them over willingly I *will* take them. You know I can do it."

Bellasiel eyes hardened but she didn't argue. She reached into her desk pulling out a heavyset ring of keys.

"We are only trying to help your brother," she told Caedmon as she handed him the keys. But Kiara couldn't believe anything she said anymore.

Caedmon didn't acknowledge the Elder's words at all. He just headed back to the dungeon.

CHAPTER EIGHTEEN

"Well? Do I get to explore on my own all the time now?" Mina asked teasingly as she looked at the scroll Arion had unfurled onto the table. They were in his chambers examining the find from the novelty shop. "Don't you think I earned it?"

Arion raised his eyebrows at her. "No," he answered flatly as he continued to examine the parchment in front of him.

Mina could barely contain her excitement. There was no doubt in her mind that they were looking at one of the lost copies of the Prophecy. What were the odds that her art fascination would lead to such a find? She knew she was gloating but she couldn't help it. And she knew Arion was pleased, too. She could tell since he was taking her jibs with good humor.

Arion finally looked up and nodded. "It is an original."

Mina hopped up and down and clapped her hands. "How do you know?"

"Well, it's on Elder parchment – but even the shopkeeper could tell that. Look at this …" he picked up the scroll and walked to the window of her room. Pulling back the curtains so the sunlight shone in, he held the scroll up to the light.

Mina gasped. In the sunlight the ink on the page grew almost translucent.

"Only copies of the Prophecy were made with this ink. It's called *solas na gealai*." Finally Arion lost the serious expression that had been on his face since leaving the shop with the scroll. He grinned at Mina. "You did it! You found the Prophecy."

Mina couldn't help beaming back. She'd felt tremendous guilt for the loss of the first copy that had been sitting on her desk in the library in Séreméla. The same scroll that Eöl Ar-Feiniel had lost his life for. If she hadn't been so stupid she would have known what that parchment had been and perhaps the old archivist would still be alive. But now that they'd found another copy of the Prophecy, they had a chance of learning what the Mark might mean.

Arion's smile faded suddenly.

"What's wrong?" Mina asked.

"Well, we have found what appears to be a complete copy of the Prophecy but we have no way of deciphering it. With Eöl Ar-Feiniel gone I don't know anyone who could read this ancient dialect."

Mina smiled tentatively. "Well, I can read a bit of it," she admitted. "Eöl Ar-Feiniel was teaching me how to read it. Apparently I had a bit of a knack for it," she added shyly.

Arion stared at her. "You had a 'knack' for it?" he asked incredulously. "Do you have any idea how complex this dialect is? And you didn't even grow up speaking the Elder language."

Mina shrugged. "It just makes sense to me." She pointed to the scroll spread between them on the table. "Eöl Ar-Feiniel said that he thought people had been misinterpreting the Prophecy for a long time. He thought that it was in part because for some reason they had relied on the *Draíodóir* to translate it for them." Mina paused remembering how angry the old archivist had been by the fact that the *Draíodóir* had full access to an Elder prophecy. She couldn't help wondering how the *Draíodóir* had gained control of the Prophecy in the first place. The one time she'd asked Eöl Ar-Feiniel about it, he'd become so furious he couldn't even speak.

Mina looked up from the parchment when she realized Arion hadn't said anything to her. He was watching her with a look of wonder on his face.

"What?" she asked.

"It's just that ..." he trailed off. "Nevermind. Show me what you understand."

Mina watched him for a moment wondering what he'd been about to say. Then she turned back to the paper in front of them. It wasn't like it was easy to decipher. Even though she understood it to some extent it still took a long time to really begin to translate it. The time that Eöl Ar-Feiniel and her had spent on the Prophecy scroll had led to very little progress. That's why they had switched to other, more accessible documents to translate at first.

Mina felt another pang of regret. At least doing the translating with Eöl Ar-Feiniel meant that the archivist was working with her and she had his expertise to lean on. It was almost as if they were completing a puzzle together. He had been so knowledgeable and the loss of him would mean more than just losing a friend.

"Mina?"

She focused on Arion's face, her thoughts pulled back from the memories of her former mentor.

"Are you alright?" he asked and Mina suddenly realized her cheeks were wet with tears.

She sniffled and nodded. "I'm sorry. I miss Eöl Ar-Feiniel."

Arion nodded in understanding. "Does it help to know that he would be very proud of you for finding the Prophecy and continuing on with the work?"

Mina smiled a little and nodded.

"Did you know him?" she asked Arion curiously.

He looked wistful. "I did. I actually spent quite a bit of time in the library in Séreméla. I found it soothing."

Mina couldn't help wondering for a moment how stressful life must have been for Arion in Meldiron's guard.

"I might be able to help you, if you show me how Eöl Ar-Feiniel guided you through the translation."

Mina looked at the parchment spread in front of them. "It took an incredible amount of time to translate even the tiniest bit," she said slowly.

Arion pulled a chair close to the table. "Good thing we seem to have an abundance of time right now, isn't it?"

#

Mina's and Arion's days were now full. They spent their mornings training and their afternoons and evenings working on the Prophecy. It was slow, arduous work and often Mina felt that she made a bit of progress in the translation only to continue and find that she had to start all over again. But she was enthralled with it. Some days she was so caught up in the challenge that she forgot to eat dinner entirely.

One late afternoon she looked up from where she was trying a variety of combinations of letters on the page to find Arion staring at her.

"What?" she asked, suddenly self conscious.

He shook his head. "It's just that you are so passionate about this work."

Mina felt her cheeks heat. "I find it intriguing. After all here is a scroll that is thousands of years old – so old that its original meaning has been lost – and yet it could hold the answers to the future of life in Five Corners. It gives me the chills to think that we are privileged to be attempting to read it!"

Arion smiled at her. "You really do love the Elder language, don't you?" he asked.

Mina nodded. She did but she didn't try to explain why. It was as though for the first time she had finally come home to her roots. She felt more comfortable with the Elder words than she did with the common tongue. In fact, since they'd started working on the Prophecy, she found that Arion and her more often spoke in the Elder tongue than in the language she'd grown up speaking with her sisters.

The first time it had happened, Arion had laughed at her and had to point it out before she realized. Now he just took it for granted that she would speak to him in his native tongue. Mina had a suspicion that he liked the fact that she was fluent in his language so quickly but she didn't talk to him about it. She thought she'd just enjoy the pleasure that lit up his face when they talked.

As for the Prophecy, it was a mystery that was proving exceedingly difficult to decipher. They'd been able to translate the first few phrases but they told them nothing. The introduction to the text was typical of any piece of Elder writing, listing the ages and the Elder royalty. That part had been easy. But what came afterward was an intricate maze of lost meaning.

But Mina wasn't going to give up. When they'd managed to eek out the meaning of just one word or phrase, Mina found herself falling asleep with a smile on her face. But in their short time with the document it was becoming clear that it would take the two of them years to fully translate it. That was unless they could find someone who was proficient in the ancient dialect and outside the *Draíodóir* ranks; Arion did not know of a single person. Even poor Eöl Ar-Feiniel only had a rudimentary understanding of it.

Still Mina was confident that there would be a way to unlock the mysteries of the ancient text. She just had to figure out how to do so.

CHAPTER NINETEEN

Thia, Xyrisse and Meldiron arrived in Bermgarten late in the afternoon four days after they found the Hunters' bodies. Meldiron had amazing senses when it came to Arion's way of thinking.

"I'm sure they wouldn't stay on the outskirts of the city," he said as they entered the busy centre. "They would go to the heart of the city where there are more people. The most heavily populated part of town is where Arion would have taken Mina."

Thia was surprised that Meldiron was so sure of himself but Xyrisse agreed with him.

The Nasseet girl nodded. "Yes, I also sense that they are closer to the center of the city," she told them.

Thia had never been in a city the size of Bermgarten. It was larger, or at least it appeared larger, than Sailsburg. She asked Meldiron about it.

He nodded, "Yes, it is bigger than Sailsberg not by much but it is a more condensed city. Because we are relatively close to the Eastern Mountains, where there are Raiders, this city is not as safe as Sailsburg and so the people tend to live closer together. Along with taking other precautions for their safety."

Thia waited for him to elaborate on his last comment but he just kept leading them through the city streets without saying anymore. She couldn't help wondering what their additional precautions might be.

Thia had never seen a city like this one. Everywhere one looked there were people and the buildings seemed to be taller than any of the buildings she'd seen in other towns and cities. People lived on top of one another more than even in the poorest areas of Sailsberg.

The streets and alleys were dirty and the smell of excrement was heavy in the air. Thia suppressed a shudder. She didn't think she'd want to be wandering around this city by herself. She was thankful that Xyrisse and Meldiron were travelling with her. And she hoped that her sister still had Arion to look after her. She didn't like to think of Mina in this city on her own. Kiara would have been able to fend for herself but Mina was a happy, daydreamer who could only too easily fall into trouble alone in such a place. Thia smiled as she thought of her sweet blond sister. Mina always thought the best of all people and, living sheltered as she had been at the Inn her whole life, Mina had no reason to believe there were ugly people in the world who would hurt her if they had a chance. She was too naïve and innocent. Even after the attack by the Hunters had left her unconscious for months, Mina was still a trusting soul. Thia couldn't imagine her ever changing.

It was almost the dinner hour when they located the inn where Mina and Arion were staying. Meldiron believed it was definitely the lodging that Arion would choose for the princess and Xyrisse sensed that Mina was in the building.

Meldiron inquired with the innkeeper and he confirmed that they were staying there. Thia felt a wave of relief wash over her. Her sister was safe and well. Meldiron had just ordered rooms for the Xyrisse, Thia, and himself when Arion and Mina walked through the entrance on their way on the dining room.

"Thia!" Mina cried in delight and swept her up into a warm embrace. "I'm so glad you're here."

Thia smiled at Mina, noting that her sister looked happy and well. Relief flooded her. Even though they'd found no indication that Mina had been hurt in the clearing, Thia had to admit that she had been concerned for her sister. The bodies of three Hunters and evidence that Arion had been injured didn't bode well for Mina's well being. But Thia could see that her fears were in vain. In fact, Mina looked almost radiant.

"You must be exhausted," Mina said as she looked closely at her. Thia resisted the urge to rub her eyes and forced a smile at her sister.

"Riding always tires me out, as you know," she admitted unwilling to let Mina know just how troubling the last few weeks had been.

Mina turned to where Meldiron and Arion were greeting one another. She put her hand on Arion's arm, Thia refrained from raising her eyebrows at the gesture of familiarity. "Thia is tired," Mina told the two Elders. "I will take her and Xyrisse to their rooms to rest and we can catch up with one another over dinner in a few hours. Thia and I will share a room, Meldiron," she added happily.

The crown prince looked like he might argue but Mina, to Thia's surprise drew herself to her full height and looked at him in almost a regal way.

"Thia is my sister and I miss her," Mina said directly. "We will want to spend some time catching up. Besides it wouldn't hurt the Crown Prince to save a few coins for later." She winked and giggled as she pulled Thia towards the stairs. Leaving Meldiron staring after her in surprise.

"You have no idea." Thia heard Arion murmur to Meldiron before Mina pulled her the rest of the way upstairs. It appeared that her sister had learned how to assert herself.

#

"So tell me everything! How did you get here?" Mina asked as soon as they had settled in her room. Xyrisse had stopped in her own bedchamber only to deposit her things, seeming to prefer the company of the women to her solitary space.

"How did you know where to find us?" Mina prodded.

Thia told her how they'd stumbled upon the camp with the dead Hunters in it.

"Meldiron knew that Arion would think to hide you in a city. And Bermgarten was the closest city."

Mina nodded and then looked at Xyrisse. "And you don't want to," she paused and swallowed nervously. "Kill me anymore?"

"The marker has faded. I was able to sense you and Arion only because of the Mark not because of the attack you suffered. With the fading my desire to kill you has also disappeared," she reassured Mina gently. "I'm sorry if I caused you any distress. I can't help what I am."

Thia spoke next. "Mina, we must speak to Meldiron and Arion about the rest of our journey."

Mina sobered for a minute. "Are we going to carry on to the Refuge now? Is it safe?"

Xyrisse nodded. "It should be safe. You are no longer any more trackable than a regular Marked One and you've been in Bermgarten long enough to have lost the trail of any Hunters that were following you."

Thia spoke up. "Mina, I wouldn't press this if it weren't for Teague."

Mina looked at her, reading the worry on her small sister's face. "What have you learned?" she asked.

But Thia shook her head. "That's what's worrying me," she admitted. "I haven't learned anything. I've still not been able to connect with Teague in the dreamwalks."

Thia didn't say the rest of what she was thinking. No one could go that long without sleep. Her fear that Teague might be dead returned but she wasn't going to share that with the others just yet. It wasn't something she wanted to say aloud.

#

Mina snuck out of the room she was sharing with Thia early the next morning. Her sister was exhausted and she didn't want to disturb her sleep. Besides, Arion and her had been on the verge of a breakthrough with the Prophecy yesterday. She couldn't wait to get back to it.

Mina slipped into Arion's room as she usually did but he wasn't sitting at the table where the Prophecy was laid out. Instead she heard voices coming from the adjoining sitting room. Elder voices.

Clearly her brother had beat her to his friend's room. She paused inside the door trying to decide if she should join them or retreat and knock. Her brother would surely find it strange that she was so comfortable entering Arion's room without first announcing herself but their routine was to meet early for training and then work on the Prophecy. In fact, other than for sleeping, Mina spent most of her time in Arion's rooms working on the manuscript.

"I can't believe it, Arion. How in the world did you find it?" She heard Meldiron ask.

Mina smiled, waiting for Arion to tell the story of how she'd discovered the shop of novelties. But instead of launching into the tale, Arion answered her brother casually. "Chance, I suppose," he said.

Mina glared in the direction of the sitting room. Why wouldn't he tell Meldiron the truth? She took a step in that direction, determined to set the record straight when her brother suddenly poked his head through the doorway.

"Ah, Mina!" Meldiron said with a smile. "Were you looking for me?"

"Um …" Mina didn't want to hurt her brother's feelings but the truth was that she wasn't looking for him. She was hoping to work on the Prophecy. She opened her mouth to say so when Arion interrupted.

"Can't you have breakfast with your sister this morning?" he asked before she could say a word. "Meldiron and I thought we'd work on translating the Prophecy."

"What?" Mina blurted out, unable to believe her ears.

Meldiron smiled at her indulgently. "I know you probably want to help, Mina, but Arion and I have been speaking the Elder language for our entire lives. We do have a better chance of making some sense of the document." He paused. "I can spend some time with you this afternoon," he offered with a warm smile.

Mina stared at her brother and then at Arion, trying to figure out what was going on here.

"Princess, you must be hungry." Arion said soothingly as he turned her gently toward the door.

Princess?! He hadn't called her that in weeks. What the heck was happening? She turned back to ask him as he pushed her out the door but before she could say a word the door was closed in her face.

#

Mina was livid about being locked out of work on the Prophecy. For some reason Arion hadn't told Meldiron about her role in deciphering the document. Nor had he told him that she had been the one to find it! Instead he kept Meldiron working on the Prophecy with him from dawn to dusk and wouldn't even let her in the room.

Thia meanwhile was becoming more and more worried about Teague. On their third day at the inn, Thia demanded to see Meldiron.

To Mina's surprise her brother and Arion joined them in their sitting room.

"We must move on," Thia said firmly in a manner that was surprising to Mina. Even more surprising was that Meldiron agreed.

"Arion and I are making no progress with the Prophecy. We can do this just as easily in the Refuge as here and, at least there we will have the assistance of Bellasiel and other Elders. Even Omen might be able to help translate."

Mina waited for Arion to say that she could help but he kept surprisingly quiet about her ability to read the Prophecy. And try as she might, he wouldn't meet her eye nor could she get him alone for even one minute to try to have him explain what was going on. He was steadfastly avoiding her. And she couldn't figure out why. Something was definitely amiss.

CHAPTER TWENTY

The night before they were scheduled to leave Bermgarten, Thia decided to try a dreamwalk. If she could find Teague and let him know they were on their way, perhaps it would ease his mind.

For some reason Thia decided to look for Teague at the meeting place she hated most. She couldn't say why she decided to go there rather than their usual meeting spot by the riverbank. Ever since she lost contact with Teague she'd been trying all the different dreamscapes to connect with him. But this was the first time she'd gone to that dark dreamscape. Every other time the dreamworld had felt empty. But this time it was almost as if she was drawn to that dark desolate place that Teague had only taken her to once before.

She'd been 10 years old the last time they had been in this dreamscape together. She had looked for Teague here when he had been in a coma. But he'd never gone back there at least not with her.

Once she made up her mind to go to a particular dreamscape her dreams shifted and she was instantly in the space. This time was no different. She simply thought of the place she hated most in her dreams and there she was.

This dreamscape Teague had created. At least that was what Thia believed. It was possible to create your own dreamscape. She'd created such places often as a child. You couldn't create people to inhabit such places but you could create the scene. She wasn't sure where characters in the dreamscapes came from but she didn't seem to ever have control over them.

When she was small she'd created a number of dreamscapes of her own. They were always the same: sunny, happy places filled with sweet smelling flowers and the buzz of insects and the sweet song of birds. But Teague's dreamscape was different. Where her creations were always filled with joy, his dreamscape was dark and frightening. It was filled with skeleton-like trees and the wind was always blowing. Thia wondered if Teague had created it as an expression of his time with the *Draíodóir*.

Regardless of why Teague had created this place, Thia only knew that it evoked fear in her. She avoided it whenever she could and Teague had never pushed her to return to this place. Feeling cold fingers of the doubt skitter over her spine, Thia stepped forward.

"Teague!" she called into the cold howling wind but her words were caught and swirled around before being blown away. "Teague!" she called again feeling hopeless but yet at the same time sensing that this dreamscape wasn't as empty as it had been the last time she been here. It was almost as if there was a sinister presence lurking behind the bare tree trunks.

Suddenly, just ahead of her, a dark shadow moved through the trees. "Teague?" she called moving in the direction that the shadow was standing. The shadow ignored her and moved deeper into the forest. Thia could hear it muttering as she followed it. It was making strange guttural noises that didn't sound quite human and yet were eerily similar to Teague's voice. She picked up her pace, ignoring the bare branches that were grabbing at her arms as if to hold her back.

And then the shadow was gone, vanished into thin air. Thia blinked unable to believe her eyes. She scanned the skeletal forest in front of her but saw nothing. She wondered if it had been Teague and if he had shifted out of this dreamscape. After a moment's hesitation, Thia decided that she would shift to the riverbank and see if she could find him there. She stopped, turned around and the shadow swooped at her out of nowhere, grabbing her by her neck and slamming her painfully against a tree trunk.

Why are you following me? It was Teague but not the Teague she knew. This Teague had wild crazed eyes, their silver color glinting with an emotion Thia couldn't name. He pulled back his lips and hissed at her as his fingers closed more tightly over her throat.

Thia tried to speak but her throat was being crushed and only gasps were escaping her lips. Her hands went to Teague's arms trying to break the grip but his arms were like steel. She began to panic and then remembered she didn't need to speak with words.

Teague let me go! His face tightened in fear and confusion as his fingers increased the pressure and Thia saw dark spots begin to fill her field of vision. *Teague, its me, Thia.*

His eyes rolled in his head crazily as he kept the grip on her neck tight. *Stop trying to get into my head.* He snarled the words and shook her slightly.

The black dots began to join and completely cloud her vision. In terror, she suddenly realized that Teague was not going to let her go. In fact he seemed determined to choke the life out of her. And if she died in a dreamscape she didn't know if she died in the waking world as well.

Suddenly desperate, Thia forced her mind to clear all the terror and fear she was feeling. She pushed the panic away and concentrated on her breathing. Once she'd calmed herself she focused on her lifeforce and felt her energy beginning to ebb. Thia built it up and then directed all of her energy into Teague.

Teague dropped Thia to the ground as he flew back across the forest floor and lay dazed and breathing heavily.

Thia gasped to get her breath back, her hands going to her throat where she could still feel his fingers around her neck.

Then she stood and walked over to Teague. He looked up at her, horror filling his face. *Thia? Thia, what have I done?* He began to sob roughly and she dropped to her knees by his side.

Sshhh, Teague, I'm alright. I'm fine.

But I tried to kill you. He moaned in anguish. *I would have killed you if you hadn't stopped me.*

Thia knew it was true but she also sensed that this was not the right time to speak of it.

Teague, I'm fine though. You didn't hurt me, she told him, ignoring the burning sensation around her neck. *Can you leave this dreamscape?* She asked, feeling the skeleton forest press down on them.

Teague looked around, his eyes darting distrustfully through the trees. *Yes, let's go to the riverbank,* he said softly, his voice almost pleading.

Cradling his head in her lap, Thia focused on shifting them to the riverbank and instantly they could feel the warm sunshine and hear the song of birds.

Teague dissolved completely into tears, his sobs filling the air. Thia sat quietly stroking his curls and at an utter loss as to what to say or do. Usually it was Teague comforting her. She'd never seen him like this before. After a time, he calmed and eventually he sat up and looked at Thia.

I haven't been able to get here, he explained. *I was stuck in that forest.*

Have you been there since we last met? Thia asked in confusion. It had been weeks since she'd seen Teague.

But he was shaking his head. *I haven't been able to sleep until ...* his voice trailed off.

But Thia focused on his words. *You haven't slept in weeks?* She asked.

Thia, I killed an innocent, Teague said suddenly, horror flooding his features.

Teague, whatever happened in that Dreamscape, wasn't real.

It wasn't in the Dreamscape, he said so softly she had to strain to catch the words, his eyes reflecting pure misery.

Fear gripped Thia's heart. *What do you mean?* She asked cautiously.

Kiara's little friend. Teague closed his eyes. *I killed a little girl, Thia. I choked the life out of her. And I felt powerful doing so.*

Thia stared at Teague, refusing to believe that he knew what he was saying. He was disoriented and confused. Even now his eyes kept shifting restlessly making him look slightly wild.

Teague, tell me everything. From the time we last met.

Teague shared with her what had been happening. He told her about Omen's sessions wherein the former *Draíodóir* helped him erect a block to the other *Draíodóir*.

But to build the wall, I had to let him into my mind, Teague explained. *And after the wall was built he continued to come into my mind and to try to unravel other connections.* He paused. *It was Omen who made it so I couldn't sleep.*

Thia listened in horror as Teague described how he'd tried to fight Omen's growing influence over his mind. Caedmon and Kiara had been searching for the Marked children and finding them. All summer they'd been bringing children to the Refuge but Teague was certain that Bellasiel and Omen were collecting the Marked children for sinister purposes.

What happened with the child? Thia asked softly. *The one you think you ...* she couldn't finish the sentence.

Teague shuddered. *Kiara should never have left her with me*, he said softly, his voice raw. *I killed her, Thia.*

How did it happen? She asked, still refusing to believe it. She knew Teague better than anyone. She *knew* he couldn't harm any living thing. To believe he would kill an innocent child was unthinkable.

He clearly didn't want to speak about it. Thia decided not to press him. They could talk about it when she arrived at the Refuge. A conversation like this was better to have in person anyway.

Teague was shaking his head. *Then they took me to the dungeons.*

Thia was shocked. *There are dungeons in the Refuge?* She asked, unable to process all he was telling her. She couldn't believe that the sanctuary Bellasiel had told them about had dungeons. That didn't sound like a sanctuary at all!

Teague nodded. *Well developed ones.*

Thia was silent for a few moments, digesting what he'd just said. Why would there be dungeons in an old mine? It didn't make sense.

Is that where you are now? She asked after a few moments.

Yes.

And you can sleep again?

Teague paused. *I don't know if it's truly sleep. When they beat me eventually I lose consciousness.*

Thia was horrified. Teague was being beaten? Why? The whole point of them going to the Refuge in the Eastern Mountains was to get help for Teague not for him to be beaten and tortured.

Who beats you Teague?

The guards.

Suddenly a look of terror crossed over Teague's face. *They are waking me, Thia.*

What? No one had ever pulled either of them from a dreamwalk. Typically they could leave when they were ready but Thia hadn't thought it was possible for either of them to be removed from a dreamwalk.

Teague, stay here with me. Look at me.

Suddenly Teague's body began to dissolve in front of her eyes.

Teague! She cried.

Come to the Refuge, Thia. Get here as fast as you can.

Teague words echoed through the riverbank and then he was gone.

#

Thia woke with a start. The sky was just brightening outside the window to the inn and Mina was snoring softly in the bed next to her.

She quietly slipped out of bed and went across the room to where a mirror was hanging on the wall.

Thia stared at her reflection in horror, her fingers tracing the purple bruises where Teague's fingers had closed around her neck. She would have to wear a scarf in order to hide the marks from her sister and the others. For reasons she didn't want to examine too closely, she wanted to keep Teague's violence from them.

Digging through her bag, Thia pondered what the marks might mean. Did it mean that the dreamwalks really were a different reality as Teague had originally suggested they might be? When they were trying to figure out what the dreamwalks meant and what they were he'd been certain the dreamwalks were a different reality. Thia had discounted that as nonsense but Teague had been really excited by the idea. Now Thia was afraid he might be right. The dreamscapes might be a different reality - a reality that was as real as this one.

Thia traced the dark purple marks, they looked just like fingers wrapped around her neck. If the dreamwalks were a different reality, then it was possible that what happened in them was real. The marks on her neck suggested that was the case. And if that were true, then was it possible to die while in a dream?

She gasped. It wasn't outside the realm of possibilities. And Teague had seemed scared while in the dreamwalk. Almost as though he'd been being hunted. Thia wondered if there were others that could enter the dreamwalks. Although Teague was the only one Thia knew who could dreamwalk, it made sense that there would be others who also could do it. Maybe there were others that were even more proficient at it than Teague and her; others who weren't necessarily good people. If there were then Teague would be in danger.

Wrapping the scarf quickly around her neck, Thia nudge Mina awake. The sooner they got to the Refuge the sooner she could help Teague. Until then she feared he would be in serious danger.

CHAPTER TWENTY-ONE

Mina watched Thia closely. Her small sister, who hated riding, was pushing them all to make this last leg of the journey as quick as possible. After a brief discussion in their room at the inn, Thia had said they had to get to the Refuge soon and then she'd spoken of Teague no more. But Mina had seen the worry that passed through Thia's golden eyes when she thought no one was looking. It was clear that, for Thia, they couldn't arrive at the Refuge fast enough.

Mina herself was looking forward to the end of their adventure. While she'd been eager to travel before Bermgarten, the joy she took in new discoveries had been tainted by her experience with Arion. She couldn't shake her anger at being shut out of the Prophecy work. And what hurt more was that she didn't understand his sudden distance. Arion was still avoiding her. She thought they were almost friends. Suddenly, she remembered what he'd told her on the beach all those weeks ago. He'd insisted that he was *not* her friend. She thought it was just his silly standoffishness because she was the Elder princess but now she wondered if he was telling her something entirely different. Did he mean that he actually could never be her friend? If that was true, then what was he to her? Whatever his role it was clear that he didn't care about her feelings.

Why she wasn't included with Meldiron to work on the Prophecy was still a mystery. She'd turned the matter over and over in her mind and the only explanation she'd come up with was that Arion didn't trust Meldiron. But that didn't make any sense whatsoever. The two Elders were close. Meldiron had once told her that Arion was the closest thing he had to a brother. And yet Mina couldn't come up with any other explanation for Arion's behavior.

Since her brother had arrived in the city, Arion had steadfastly avoided her. Even while they travelled, she noticed that he was the first to volunteer to go ahead and scout their path. At night he always made sure his sleeping roll was on the opposite side of camp from her own. And he avoided her eyes constantly. Mina couldn't help being hurt. And her hurt quickly escalated to anger. As a result she had distanced herself from

Meldiron. Which perhaps was not fair but her brother's happy demeanor just made her more frustrated.

At first Meldiron tried to start conversations with her but when she often refused to engage in an extended dialogue him, he began to take the hint and started to spend most of his time speaking to Xyrisse. Mina took slim satisfaction from the fact that Meldiron and Arion rarely exchanged words for some reason. Mina was beginning to wonder if they'd argued and if that was why Meldiron had agreed so readily to starting on the road to the Eastern Mountains.

One night when the camp was asleep except for Meldiron and Arion, who were on guard duty, Mina was woken by the sound of angry voices. She listened for a moment and realized that the two of them were arguing in the Elder language. Realizing she was the only one in the camp who could understand them, she rolled over and listened intently.

"Meldiron, I'm telling you that we shouldn't trust Bellasiel and Omen so readily. They were very much in the confidence of the Elder council."

"But Bellasiel can be trusted, Arion. I'm sure of it."

"You are sure of it? I am closer to her than you, practically her son and I am not sure of it." Arion said bitterly. "You do not know all she has done."

Meldiron sounded impatient. "Arion, Bellasiel saved your life once. You are not going to forgive her for not approving an ill-fated marriage when you were no more than a boy?"

"That is not why I question her loyalties," Arion cut in.

"It is part of it though. You have never forgiven her for her being against your union with Glassada."

Mina held her breath not wanting to miss anything from this exchange. Arion had a girlfriend? She ignored the sudden pricking around her heart.

"Bellasiel was right about Glassada. I would have come to the same conclusion if she'd given me time to do so myself," Arion insisted reasonably. "The problem with Bellasiel is that she can't let anyone else come to their own conclusions. She has to be in charge. But what I'm concerned about here is far more important than a lover. It is the Prophecy, Meldiron. We have to be careful."

"We need help translating it, Arion. If we don't trust Bellasiel then who are we going to trust?"

Arion was silent. Mina longed to speak up but something held her back.

"Just remember your primary job is not to take care of the Prophecy. I can handle that. Your job is as *Coimirceoir* to the Banphrionsa. I won't have my sister in danger."

Mina wrinkled her forehead. What was this? *Coimirceoir* meant guardian or protector in the Elder language and Eöl Ar-Feiniel had always called her Banphrionsa. Did that mean Arion was charged with protecting her?

"I know my duty," Arion answered quietly.

"Well, remember it and let me worry about the Prophecy."

The conversation ended then but Mina could tell neither man was happy. She turned their words over in her head trying to come to a conclusion as to what they meant but after a long day in the saddle, sleep was pulling at her. Filing that information away for later inspection, Mina let herself be claimed by a deep slumber.

#

A few days later when they stopped for camp, Mina overheard Meldiron telling Thia that they were only about two days from the Refuge now. They were camping just off the road in a small copse of trees. Mina left Meldiron and Thia setting up camp. Xyrisse had gone hunting for dinner as she often did. Her Hunter skills served her well when it came to the task of keeping their bellies full and Xyrisse didn't seem to mind killing animals. Mina headed towards the river, with the intention of splashing some cool water on her face after the long dusty ride.

As she emerged on the riverbank she saw Arion dunking his head in the water. Sensing an opportunity to figure out what was going on, Mina headed in his direction. But when she was within speaking distance, Arion quickly moved away from her.

"Princess. I will give you some privacy," he said stiffly, his eyes focused on some spot above her left ear.

"Oh no you don't. And stop with the "princess" crap, too," she spat, "you have some serious explaining to do."

Arion moved to stand in front of her. "Keep your voice down, Princess," he said, his eyes flashing a warning at her.

Mina opened her mouth but he pressed his fingers to her lips. The warmth of them momentarily caused her to swallow her words. "Please, Mina," he said softly.

She looked up at his pale eyes. The expression in them was pleading with her to understand. But she didn't understand. She had no idea what was going on here and he couldn't just expect her to stop questioning.

She opened her mouth to tell him so when he suddenly bent his head and pressed his lips to hers.

Startled Mina forgot what she was going to say. Arion's lips were gentle and yet she liked how they fit to her own. She sighed and closed her eyes, letting herself get lost in the moment of her first kiss.

When he stiffened and pulled away, Mina was confused. Until she heard her brother's angry voice. She turned her head.

"Arion, what are you doing?" Meldiron was striding down the riverbank toward them all regal Elder prince.

Mina turned back to Arion. What was he up to? Anger stabbed at her. He staged that kiss and she fell for it. She was so stupid. And now he was avoiding her eyes again.

"What is going on here?" Meldiron asked when he arrived where they were standing.

"Exactly," Mina started to say, wondering just what game Arion was playing but before she could say more her brother had cut her off.

"Minathrial, go back to the camp. I will deal with this," he ordered.

Mina was tempted to argue but the look on her brother's face was one she'd never seen before. He was livid. Why? Just because Arion kissed her? It seemed absurd. The kiss wasn't the big deal but the fact that he'd not meant it was.

And Arion looked a little too pleased with himself.

Mina started on the trail back to camp but as soon as she disappeared from sight, she hid in some underbrush so she could listen to their conversation. She gasped in shock as Meldiron's hand struck Arion's cheek and Arion stood stiffly but did not fight back.

"How long has this being going on with my sister?" Meldiron demanded.

Arion smirked. "How long do you think?" he asked in a mocking tone.

"Arion why?" Meldiron asked, pain in his voice. "You know the Elder rules with respect to the Banphrionsa. Why would you violate them? Especially when you are her *Coimirceoir*."

There was that word again. Mina grimaced but filed the information away for next time she spoke to Arion alone. She wanted to know what the duties of a *Coimirceoir* might be. She knew that Brijit, her mother, and her husband Weylon has been *Coimirceoirí* or Guardians of the Elders but a *Coimirceoir* sounded a bit different. Pushing her thoughts aside she shifted her attention back to the exchange taking place below.

Arion shrugged. "I'm not who you think I am Meldiron. The Banphrionsa has more appeal than being your sidekick. You take traditions too seriously. You sister is a bit more … adverturous."

Mina frowned. Why was Arion goading her brother?

"Leave." Meldiron said coldly as he turned his back to Arion. "You have ten minutes to collect your things and leave camp. I don't want you near my sister again."

Arion didn't argue, he didn't even look surprised. He merely turned and hiked back toward camp. He paused slightly when he was parallel to where Mina was hiding and seemed to look directly at her but she couldn't read his expression. And then he was gone.

#

When Mina came out of her hiding place and made her way back to camp, she found that there was no trace of Arion remaining. He hadn't wasted any time in leaving.

Blinking back tears she went to her tent to see if he'd left a note for her but of course there was nothing. What had she been thinking? She was acting no better than Sukey Greensleeves, their silly serving girl back at the Inn who had fallen for any mildly attractive young man who paid her attention. Was Mina doing the same with Arion?

No, she told herself. She didn't care for Arion in that way. Although she did have to admit that the kiss was quite lovely. Especially for a first kiss, which Kiara had told her were always horrid. What hurt about Arion was the fact that she had believe he was her friend and he clearly had never felt that way about her. He had just been fulfilling his duty as *Coimirceoir* whatever that was.

What had happened to him? Arion was acting completely out of character ever since Meldiron had arrived. And their conversation at the riverbank made no sense to her at all.

He had let her brother believe that there was something more going on between them than there actually was. Why would he do such a thing? And she was certain the kiss, as pleasant as it had been, was staged for her brother's sake not for her own. Still she couldn't believe he had just left without saying goodbye.

Miserably she went to join the others for dinner. Thia asked where Arion was and Meldiron said he'd gone back to Séreméla on Elder business. Thia looked like she would question this information but then she shrugged and returned to her tea and staring into the fire. Mina had noticed that her sister hadn't been eating much since they'd left Bermgarten. Thia was obviously worried about Teague but she definitely didn't want to talk about it to anyone. Mina was happy they were only two days away from him.

"What business?" Mina asked when it seemed that no one would question her brother about Arion.

"Elder business, Minathrial," Meldiron answered coldly. "I think you know what it's about."

Then he stood and left the warmth of the fire. Mina felt a stab of hurt and then anger. Her brother hadn't even asked for her side of what had happened on the riverbank. And Arion appeared to be happy to let Meldiron believe the worse. She had to wonder what game was Arion playing?

#

It was deep night when Mina woke to a hand covering her mouth. She tried to scream but her voice was completely muffled.

"Ssshh, Mina, it's me." Arion's voice was warm in her ear. Mina didn't know if she was angry or happy that he'd come back for her. "You must come quietly and not question me until we are away from here."

Frustration warred with curiosity and the latter won. Shrugging in to her cloak, Mina followed Arion. He stooped to pick up her bags but before she could ask why they would need her things, he reached back and grasped her hand with one of his strong ones and led her through the blackness of night.

Mina was surprised to find that he had tethered both her mare and his mount close to camp. She opened her mouth to ask what was going on and saw Arion shake his head slightly, then offer her a leg up onto her horse.

Without arguing Mina mounted the mare and followed him away from camp. She wanted to get some answers and this might be the only chance she would have to do so.

Arion was taking no chances. He kept them riding for more than an hour and then led her off the road into a small moonlit clearing in the forest.

He turned to her. "I know you must be wondering what is going on."

"You think?" Mina asked, unable to keep the anger from her words.

"I'm sorry. I didn't expect Meldiron to find us so quickly in Bermgarten," he said as if that explained everything.

Mina stared at him waiting for him to go on. When he remained silent in the darkness with only the palest of moonlight accenting his features, she prodded him. "Arion, am I supposed to understand why we would be hiding from my brother? What is going on? You've been acting strange ever since he arrived in Bermgarten. You didn't even let me near the Prophecy after he came. And what was that nonsense on the riverbank?"

Arion sighed. "I knew that the one way to get Meldiron to eject me from the group was if I made him think we were involved romantically. I'm sorry if that upset you." He paused.

Mina bit her lip. It actually hadn't upset her. She thought it was rather nice but *he* obviously didn't! But she wasn't going to initiate a discussion about it.

"Why did you want Meldiron to force you to leave?" she asked instead focusing on the more important question.

Arion dismounted from his horse and led it further into the clearing. Mina followed but she stayed in the saddle. He turned and she could just barely see his face in the shadows cast by the trees.

"Mina, we can't let Meldiron get to the Refuge with the Prophecy."

"Why?"

"Because it must not ever fall into the hands of Bellasiel and Omen."

Mina stared. Bellasiel had saved Arion's life when he was a child. She couldn't believe what he was saying. But she remembered the conversation she'd overheard a few nights before.

"And it's even more important that they don't get you under their control?"

Under their control? Now what was he talking about? "I don't understand," she said in frustration. "Quit talking in riddles and just explain to me what is going on."

Arion shook his head. "I keep forgetting how little you know about your role in all of this. If you'd been raised in Séreméla you would understand better."

"Then explain it," Mina cut in, her frustration boiling over.

"We don't have time for me to explain it now. We have to keep moving. As soon as Meldiron discovers that both you and the Prophecy are gone, he will start looking for us. Can you trust me for now, Mina?"

Mina stared at Arion in the darkness. He was asking a lot of her. He was asking her to trust him and go against her brother.

But Meldiron was a brother she hardly knew. Even so she loved him and trusted him. How could Arion, who was supposed to be his closest friend, now be asking her to turn her back on him?

"I don't know if I can, Arion. Meldiron would never do anything to harm me." In fact it was just the opposite. Meldiron would do anything to help her.

"That's true," he quickly agreed, much to her surprise. "But he doesn't know the danger he is putting you in. The danger he is leading all of us into with the Prophecy and you in hand. Mina, I promise you I will explain but we have to keep going. It will be dawn in less than four hours and if we haven't put some serious distance between us, Meldiron will find us."

Mina bit her lip. This was not a decision she wanted to make. But Arion had never lied to her or done anything to make her think she couldn't trust him. In fact, he'd trained her to be a more self-sufficient person. And she thought he was her friend. She owed it to him to trust him at least until she'd heard him out.

"Okay," she nodded. "But you need to tell me everything as soon as you can. And if after hearing your side of the story I don't agree with your plan, you have to promise me that you will take me back to Meldiron."

"Okay," he agreed, the relief clear in his voice. He obviously would not have tried to stop her if she'd returned to camp.

With one more look over her shoulder Mina followed Arion back onto the road, noting that they were going directly westward in the opposite direction of the Eastern Mountains.

CHAPTER TWENTY-TWO

The giant mountain loomed sinisterly ahead of them. Thia stared at its hulking bulk. Somewhere, beyond the gaping mouth to the mines, was Teague. She swallowed the lump that had formed in her throat, fear making her stomach clench. She knew Teague was in some kind of danger, but she didn't know what to expect.

She felt like she didn't know what to expect from almost every side now. She didn't even want to think about how she was going to explain to Kiara that they'd lost Mina. It still hurt to think back to that morning.

Arion had obviously snuck back into the camp and taken her. Meldiron found his footprint right outside Mina's tent. But what was more painful was the fact that there was no sign of a struggle. Meaning that Mina had gone willingly.

And even more disturbing was that they'd taken the Prophecy with them. Why, Thia couldn't say but Meldiron was sure that Arion was working for the Enemy. He'd come up with a theory that Arion had been compromised while separated from them in Sailsburg. Which would mean that Mina was in danger. Except …

Thia wasn't so sure this was true. She knew Mina better than Meldiron did and she didn't think her sister would be so easily tricked. If anything Mina would question Arion so much it would slow them down. Her sister had always been inquisitive and, while too trusting at times, she wouldn't abandon Thia without a good reason.

Besides Thia remembered the way Arion's harsh Elder features had always softened when he looked at Mina. No she didn't think he was working for the Enemy. But why he'd taken Mina and the Prophecy and disappeared still wasn't clear.

Meldiron had taken Xyrisse and pursued Arion and Mina for two days. When they returned to camp, they were alone. And Thia had managed to convince them to continue to the Refuge where they could get reinforcements and continue their search. Now they were here.

Ignoring the fatigue that was pulling at her from every side, Thia dismounted and narrowed her eyes as she studied the mountain in front of her. Fall was whispering through the tall grasses on either side of the path that lead to the entrance, cold fingers of winter not far off now. But it was nothing like the bitter cold she'd experienced on the Northern Mountains. Still, she had the odd sense that this Eastern Mountain range was less welcoming than frigid climes of the Northern range. A shiver ran down her back as she studied the gaping manmade entry to the mountain. Foreboding weighed heavy in her gut and suddenly she was very afraid.

Swallowing her fear, Thia led the others to the entrance of the Refuge. They must have been spotted climbing the trail to the mountain door because she hadn't taken more than two steps inside before Kiara swept her up in her arms, exclaiming how thrilled she was to see her.

Thia let her sister swing her around also happy to see Kiara but at the same time her thoughts turned Teague. She wondered what had become of him. She could see Caedmon hovering silently in the passageway behind her sister but there was no sign of Teague. Thia wasn't surprised. She felt in her heart that something very bad had happened.

Kiara let her go and looked over her shoulder expectantly. A look of concern crossed over her face when their blond sister was nowhere to be seen.

"Mina?"

Thia shook her head miserably. And Meldiron stepped forward.

"Arion has kidnapped her," he said bluntly.

"What?!" Kiara exclaimed, rage infusing her frame.

"I don't know why but I think they have become romantically involved. He knows this goes against his duty as her *Coimirceoir* and Arion has always been loyal. This makes little sense. I forbade him to be with her and sent him from our camp. He snuck back in the night and took her."

"We need to go after them," Kiara stated.

Thia caught her sister's eye. "There was no sign of a struggle from Mina's tent," she noted quietly.

Understanding flashed across Kiara's face.

"Perhaps we should discuss plans before we charge across the Five Corners," Kiara amended as she turned to Meldiron. Her sister knew that if Mina hadn't have wanted to go with Arion she wouldn't have gone.

Ignoring Meldiron's budding plans to put together a pursuit team, Thia turned to Caedmon. "Where is he?" she asked softly, pain making her voice hoarse.

Caedmon didn't answer her. His face was grim. "Come," he said quietly as he led her away from the others.

Thia followed him, unable to speak despite the thousand questions that were pressing up through her mind.

Caedmon led her down a steep stairway. As the path sunk into the earth, Thia's heart began to hammer. She was not afraid of being below ground - she had spent months with the People the previous year. But there was something different about this place. It reeked of corruption. The mine walls became damp and musty the further they descended into the earth. While the Underground felt organic and alive, this place felt corrupted and filled with the forewarning of death. Why was Teague in such a place? Thia felt sick just thinking about happy-go-lucky Teague in this place of darkness.

After they had descended for what seemed like far too long, Caedmon turned right and led her into a dark chamber, lit dimly by a few torches. Across one wall were a series of cells, clearly built to hold prisoners. Only one was occupied and at first Thia didn't recognize the bundle of rags huddling in the corner. As Caedmon unlocked the cell, it suddenly hit her. That bundle was Teague.

As the door clattered open, Teague jerked his head and squinted into the torchlight.

Thia gasped. He had lost so much weight his body now resembled a skeleton clothed in filthy ripped clothing. His hair had grown and hung in dirty matted curls around his painfully thin face. But it was his eyes, darting around the darkness, glinting in a dangerous way that hit Thia the hardest.

What had happened to Teague? Tears filled her eyes, as a band of pain tightened around her chest.

He squinted at them and then looked away muttering under his breath.

Thia looked at Caedmon in concern.

"He doesn't recognize any of us anymore," Caedmon admitted.

"Why is he locked down here?" she choked out.

"We left the door unlocked at first but last week he attacked the guard when he brought him his dinner. Ripped his ear off." Caedmon closed his eyes for a moment and Thia could see how much this was paining him. "Bellasiel wanted him chained to the wall." He nodded toward the chains that hung from the wall.

Thia stared at them in horror. What did Caedmon mean? Had Teague been chained up?

"I would not let her do that to him again," Caedmon said, his voice hoarse with emotion. "Instead I've been staying with him. When I must leave I lock the cell." He paused and looked at her. "Not because I fear Teague escaping but because I don't trust Omen to stay away from him."

Thia stared at him in surprise. "I thought Omen was helping him?" she said softly even as she remembered Teague's words from their last dreamwalk.

"So did we - at first." Caedmon cursed under his breath. "If I'd just paid more attention to what was happening here instead of recruiting more children for Bellasiel's army."

Thia shook her head in confusion. What army? Clearly there was much more going on at the Refuge than she anticipated even with Teague's warning.

Caedmon shook his head. "Never mind. I'm sure Kiara will fill you in on the details."

Bewildered but nodding anyway Thia turned back to where Teague was still huddled in the corner. He was rocking slightly now, his muttering had taken on a rhythmic quality but it was tinged with such pain. She stepped toward him but Caedmon stopped her with a large hand on her arm.

"I don't think that's wise, Thia. Teague is not himself and he has already killed a child not much larger than you."

Thia shook her head. Teague would not hurt her. She was sure of that.

"Let me go, Caedmon. I know the risk. It is my choice."

She gently removed his hand from her arm and walked over to where Teague was rocking. She crouched down in front of him. "Teague?" she said softly. There was no response. His mutterings continued as if he hadn't heard her.

"Teague?" she said again, louder this time. But it was to no avail. The voices in his head were louder than her spoken word. Thia decided to become one of those voices.

Teague.

His eyes flashed to her face.

"You!" He growled aloud before he launched himself at her, his hands clamped around her throat, as they had in the dreamscape.

Thia felt the electric charge from him resonate from his hands. She vaguely heard Caedmon moving behind her and then she was falling into a vision. The first one she'd had in months.

Teague standing in front of a child army, laughing manically as they advanced on helpless peasants. Bellasiel smiling with Omen over plans on a table. Mina with a terribly scarred man, a crown glinting on her golden curls. Meldiron and Xyrisse on a ship with the ocean spray sparkling on their skin. Kiara, naked and scarred, blood dripping down her legs.

Thia awoke from the vision suddenly, her head throbbing and her throat aching for breath. Kiara was cradling her head in her knee while Meldiron and Caedmon chained a sobbing Teague to the wall.

"Thia, I'm sorry, I didn't know," Teague moaned, his silver eyes pleading with her.

Thia sat up.

"Careful, darling, you've had a vision."

Thia shook her head, pushing her sister away and moved to stand in front of Teague. She'd been so stupid not to anticipate the energy from Teague. It had been so long since he'd been able to throw her into a vision. Now he felt guilty. Her heart ached as he sobbed on the wall.

"Shhh," she said softly as she cupped his cheek, this time she controlled the sparks that erupted sending them back to Teague. "I know you wouldn't harm me on purpose. I should have been prepared."

She turned to Caedmon.

"Unchain him."

Kiara shook her head. "Thia, you saw firsthand how unstable he is. It's not safe –"

"It's inhumane to keep him chained up," Thia turned on her sister savagely.

Thia, they're right.

Thia turned back to see Teague watching her, tears glimmering in his silver eyes. He shook his head.

I'm sorry.

No, I will not let you live like this.

Then kill me.

His words cut her to the core. *What are you saying?*

I can't control these voices in my head. I don't know how to do it. Right now I'm here. I'm me. But ...

"Alright. I have a compromise to suggest," Thia said aloud. "Teague will not be chained to a wall."

She held up her hand as the others protested.

"No. Listen. He can have his freedom in the cell. But Caedmon will keep the door locked. And only Caedmon will enter until we have a plan to help Teague regain himself." Thia closed her eyes, fatigue pulling at her.

"You need rest," Meldiron observed.

Thia nodded. She did - she needed to sleep after her vision. *Teague,* she called out.

Thia go. I will be fine for a while.

I will find a way to help you, she vowed.

But Teague did not reply. He closed his eyes and let himself slump to the floor as Caedmon unchained him. Thia had never seen such a physical symbol of hopelessness. She couldn't let Teague give up. She wouldn't.

#

"Do you really truly believe that Bellasiel is working against us?" Meldiron asked Caedmon and Kiara, disbelief clear in his voice.

Kiara watched as the Elder struggled with story that Caedmon and her had shared with him. Thia was still sleeping, she hadn't yet told them about her vision but Kiara knew it would be an important one. And in the meantime, Caedmon and her had shared their concerns with the others.

"I refuse to believe it's true," Meldiron said vehemently. "Why would Bellasiel work against us?" But there was a hint of doubt in his voice.

"Regardless of past relationships, we need to consider that Bellasiel may not as impartial as we had first thought," Caedmon said reasonably. "Much has happened while you were away."

"Tell us again what Bellasiel's reaction was when the girl was killed." Meldiron instructed Kiara.

Kiara recounted all that had happened with Teague and Bellasiel since she arrived from the last scouting trip. She also told them about her distrust of the former *Draíodóir* named Omen.

"I can't put my finger on it," Kiara said, "But there's something about that man that I don't trust. And Teague became extremely agitated when he came into the room." She paused for a moment, her eyes distant.

"It was almost as if Omen was violating Teague in some way." Kiara shook her head. "It sounds crazy but that's the only way I can describe it."

"What about Bellasiel?" Meldiron asked.

"Bellasiel has been extremely uncoorporative since we arrived. She was insistent that Teague be locked up stating that he was a danger to others."

"Well, he has hardly proven himself innocent there," Meldiron interrupted.

But Kiara shook her head. "I know but it was how insistent she was about it. But beyond Teague it's her fixation with the Marked children."

Meldiron looked her sharply. "What do you mean?"

But it was Caedmon who spoke up. "It is like she is obsessed with finding more of them. She has been trying to get Kiara and I to fit in another scouting mission before the winter sets in."

"That's crazy," Xyrisse said suddenly, speaking for the first time. "Winter will come quickly to these mountains."

Kiara nodded. "Yes, but Bellasiel wants more of the children and I think she would be happy to have Caedmon and I out of the picture for a while."

"Why?" Meldiron asked impatiently. His disbelief was clear in his voice.

"So that Omen can have access to my brother again," Caedmon answered.

Kiara nodded. "It's as if Teague is an unfinished project to them. They keep saying it's to keep the *Draíodóir* away -"

"Well that *is* a noble cause," Meldiron argued but his reasons were starting to sound desperate.

"Perhaps," Kiara conceded, "but not to the extent they are pushing it."

There was movement at the door to the chamber. Mina turned and saw Thia entering leaning heavily on the frame of the door.

"Thia, you should be resting," Kiara told her little sister. But Thia shook her head despite the lines of fatigue that were clear on her face.

"We need to leave this place and take Teague with us," she told them.

"Winter is almost upon the mountains and you are suggesting we leave?" Meldiron asked incredulously. "Why?"

"I fear we are all in danger here."

#

Thia sat down on a chair and accepted a glass of water from Xyrisse before she continued.

"I had a vision with my seizure," she said softly, knowing that this would be no surprise to her sister.

"What did you see?" Kiara asked urgently.

Thia thought back to the jumble of visions that had come to her. Some she didn't understand - like Mina and the crown. Others she didn't think were important enough to share - at least not for the discomfort they would cause others. Xyrisse and Meldiron, for example. And she didn't want to scare Kiara …

"This was one of the most complex visions I've had since we ran," she explained slowly. "Teague must not stay here - Omen and Bellasiel will use him for wicked purposes if we leave them to it."

"I knew they were up to no good. We should never have trusted that woman," Kiara said vehemently.

Meldiron stood and looked like he would leave the room.

"Wait," Thia said, her quiet voice clear despite the others' exclamations over Kiara's words. "I do not think Bellasiel is evil. I'm not sure about Omen. Bellasiel believes she is acting in the best interest of the Five Corners. And she is not acting alone."

There was silence at Thia's last words.

"I do not know who she is acting with but first and foremost we need to get help for Teague."

"And how do you propose we do that?" Caedmon asked.

Thia took a deep breath. "We must take him to Celeste in the Underground."

Again the others began to argue and talk at once. Thia waited for them to fall silent. She was still tired from her vision and didn't have the energy to attempt to speak over them.

"I've been thinking about this. The *Draíodóir* did this to him. Celeste and the People are the only ones who have the skill to help him. And more importantly," Thia paused until they were all looking at her, "We can trust them."

"Are you certain of that?" Meldiron asked.

Thia didn't hesitate. "Yes. They have no interest in rejoining what they call the Upper World. But they do have an interest in Teague and I as Halflings. They will do anything they can to make him well again."

"But last time you said you became sick when you were in the Underground," Kiara pointed out.

Thia nodded. "We did but not immediately. We were there for months before we started to exhibit signs of sickness. I'm hoping Teague will be well before he becomes ill."

Caedmon spoke then. "If it will help Teague then we must try. Nothing here will help him."

Thia nodded.

"Well, it's good in theory but how do you propose we transport him there?" Kiara asked. "We agree, for the most part." She looked at Meldiron. "That we can't trust Omen with Teague. But how are we going to travel with him."

Thia licked her lips. She had given this some thought. "We can sedate him. I can mix a tonic that will keep him asleep for most of the journey. But that isn't our greatest challenge."

All eyes turned to her again. "I don't know where an entrance to the Underground might be," she admitted.

"What?" Kiara asked. The others looked equally confused.

"Or I should say, a safe entrance." Thia shook her head. "You remember the passage in the Northern Mountains was buried beneath a landslide. I'm assuming that entrance is still blocked. The only other entrance I know of is the one near Séreméla and that one is not safe to enter as it is far too close to the Valley where we are still outlaws."

There was silence in the room as her words sunk in. The Kiara spoke up.

"I may have another option," she said slowly. She turned to Caedmon. "The *manach* may be able to help us?"

"The mystic monks?" Meldiron interrupted. "Do they even exist?"

"They do exist," Caedmon said drily. "I thought they were just a nursery tale as well until I saw them with my own eyes."

"And what makes you think they would help us?" Xyrisse asked.

Thia watched as Kiara hesitated for a moment. "I can't guarantee that they will help us," Kiara admitted. "But they did help Caedmon and I before and they expressed their concern for the Marked Ones at that time. I believe they will help us. But that is not our biggest problem in soliciting their aid."

"What is?" Thia asked.

Kiara sighed. "Their location. There is a reason they are considered characters in folktales. They live deep in the Northern

Mountains on the edge of the great glacier. Caedmon and I only found them by chance."

Caedmon nodded in agreement. "Not only that, winter is fast approaching. Kiara and I barely made it to the Valley last year. The *manach* did aid us but even so - getting to them and then back at this time of year would be close to impossible even for us." He looked at Thia. "You would not have made the trip last time and there is no way that a sedated Teague could be carried to them."

Xyrisse surprised them by speaking up. "There is another way," she said softly. "You forget that I am able to teleport. I could take one, possibly two, there and back without the hardship of a journey."

"You can do that?" Thia asked.

Xyrisse nodded. "Hunters are able to transport their prey. I could easily transport you to these *manach*."

Thia didn't like being compared to prey but what choice did they have? And she did trust Xyrisse.

"But I don't know them at all. Either Kiara or Caedmon would have to come with us."

Xyrisse looked at them both. "Kiara I could take. Caedmon would be too much, I fear."

"One of us should stay here and watch over Teague at any rate," Kiara put in.

"Okay. When do we leave?"

CHAPTER TWENTY-THREE

It was decided that they would leave after Thia had recovered completely from her seizure. While she normally only needed a day to recover, the seizures that were induced by Teague took longer to get over. Thia was annoyed at herself because she should have been ready for the reaction she had to Teague. It wasn't until she'd spent time in the Underground that she'd learned to control it. Teague, in fact, usually wore gloves but they seem to have been taken away from him. Or he may have stopped wearing them on purpose, a little voice inside her head reminded her.

But there were other issues to deal with before Thia and Kiara could make the trip to the *manach* with Xyrisse. Bellasiel was not happy about Mina and Arion being missing.

"Why did you not go after them?" she asked Meldiron and Thia was surprised by the tone in the Elder's voice. She did not sound like someone speaking to her Crown Prince.

"I did go after them but they had too much of a lead on us," he told her.

Bellasiel looked dubious. "You had a Hunter with you. Could she not have tracked them?"

"Xyrisse was recovering from injuries so severe she almost died," Thia broke in. "There was no way she would be able to Hunt, even if she wanted to."

Bellasiel remained unconvinced. She spoke about putting together a recovery team but to Thia's surprise, Meldiron seemed less keen on the idea than he had been when they first arrived at the Refuge.

Later in Caedmon's chambers, where they were holding a private meeting, he expressed his own suspicion of Bellasiel.

"Arion told me that he did not trust Bellasiel and Omen with the Prophecy or with Mina. I didn't believe him but now that I'm here and I see what is happening …" he paused, his shoulders slumping for a moment, "I see I should have given his words more credence."

Thia smiled at him encouragingly. "Arion will forgive you," she assured him.

Meldiron sighed. "He isn't in a relationship with your sister, is he?"

Thia wasn't sure about that. She thought the Elder had seemed very fond of Mina for someone who was not in a relationship. But she kept her thoughts to herself.

"Where do you think they may have gone?" she asked instead.

Meldiron shook his head. "I have no idea. But I suspect Arion counted on that. Clearly he has not trusted me as I have trusted him." Sadness was etched on his handsome features. Xyrisse came and stood beside him. She tentatively placed her translucent hand on his shoulder. Meldiron smiled sadly at her.

"Perhaps he did not trust you with that information not because he doubted you, but because he was protecting you," Caedmon spoke from the corner. Thia wondered what Teague's brother might know about it but she didn't ask him directly.

"At any rate, I don't think we should send a party after Mina and Arion. He will protect her with his life. Of that at least I'm certain. And I think my sister will be safer away from the Refuge."

And with that, they were once again meeting in secret and trusting no one who didn't have the Mark.

#

While Thia continued to recover they came to a rudimentary agreement about how the group would move forward. It was obvious to everyone that Bellasiel would not allow Teague to be taken from the Refuge. So they decided to tell her nothing about their plans for the moment. After all, they weren't even sure the *manach* would help them.

When it came time to move Teague to the Underground, they would do so without informing Bellasiel. Kiara had suggested that Xyrisse move Teague but she quickly reminded them of Teague's effect on a Hunter.

"I wish I could help but one who has been trained as a *Draíodóir* is immune to my talents. And a *Draíodóir* would be dangerous to me. I do want to help but I'm afraid I can't move your friend."

They had decided to worry about the logistics of moving Teague when the time came. In the meantime, Thia was trying to learn as much about the *manach* as she could from Kiara but her sister was not very forthcoming with information.

"Thia, I'm not trying to be difficult, I just don't remember a lot of it. All I know is that I felt safe with them."

"But how do you know they can help us?" Thia insisted.

Kiara shook her head. "I can't explain it, I just have a hunch. They warned Caedmon and I about the Elders last time we were there. It was like they knew something was going to happen to us."

This was the first time Kiara had mentioned that. "What did they say?"

But her sister shook her head. "It wasn't anything specific. They just told us not to trust them and that our destiny was to save the Marked Ones. That was all."

Thia thought about that. It was obvious that the Elders had been behind much of the extermination of the Marked Ones that had been happening in the Five Corners. Now it sounded as though the *manach* knew more than they did about the Elder's intentions. If nothing else it would be worth a visit to them.

Before they left to see the *manach*, Thia wanted to see Teague one more time. Kiara had objected but Thia was firm. She would see him again even if it meant Caedmon had to supervise them and she had to remain outside the locked cell.

When she arrived in the dungeons, Teague was in the same place as last time but he wasn't muttering to himself and he looked less tortured than the last time she'd seen him.

Teague.

He looked at her and smiled. *You came back.* He walked closer to her studying her through the bars.

Of course I came back.

Are you alright, Thia?

She saw the worry and panic in his eyes. *Teague I'm fine. And the vision that came with the seizure made a few things clearer.* But it made more things less clear, a little voice reminded her. Thia pushed the wayward thought aside. *We are going to get you some help and get you out of here.*

A sad expression passed over his face. *Do you really believe that is possible?*

Of course I do! Teague whatever Omen did to you can be undone. I'm sure of it. I'm working on taking you to Celeste.

Teague's expression cleared. *The Underground?*

Thia nodded. *I'm sure they will have a way to break the spell that's haunting you. I have to go for a few days but when I come back we'll be able to take you to Celeste.*

Hope ebbed into Teague's silver eyes. He nodded.

Don't give up, Thia told him. Then she left before he saw the tears in her eyes. She would find a way to help him. She had to.

#

Kiara glanced warily at Xyrisse as they prepared to teleport to the *manach*.

"Are you certain you can do this?" she asked the Hunter suspiciously. Kiara still wasn't convinced that Xyrisse was on their side. Thia had explained how they'd found her close to death in the dunes, abandoned by her own people for her refusal to kill Marked children but Kiara couldn't shake her unease around her. She found her red eyes unsettling. And Xyrisse was always listening. She could easily be a spy. What if this whole teleporting thing was a way to get rid of Thia and herself?

Xyrisse looked steadily at Kiara with her blood-tinged eyes. "You do not trust me," she noted, her rasping voice soft. "I understand that. Perhaps one day you will feel otherwise. But I assure you that this can, and will, work. Provided you have given me an accurate description of where we are going and you promise to keep your mind open."

Kiara nodded reluctantly. For the teleport to work, Xyrisse had explained that Kiara and her would have to link minds. Xyrisse had never been to the *manach*'s domain so she needed to link with someone who had been there for them to teleport safely and accurately. Kiara understood the theory behind this - it made sense. Still she wasn't thrilled to be having a Hunter in her head.

Caedmon drew her aside. "Be careful," he said gruffly.

Kiara looked up at him. He was worried for her she suddenly realized. Warmth filled her for a moment. Caedmon and her had not had any time alone since he'd returned from his mysterious trip - a trip he still hadn't told her the reason behind.

Kiara missed him and she'd started to worry that their relationship might be over. But the fear reflected in Caedmon's dark eyes made her think otherwise.

"I love you," she whispered.

He pulled her close and held her tightly. "I love you, too," he mumbled into her hair. Kiara suppressed a smile. Caedmon had never been good at talking about his feelings. In fact, he made her look like an expert at sharing her feelings, which was laughable when compared to her sisters. She pulled away slightly and stood on her toes before pressing her lips against his. Caedmon responded with a kiss so searing Kiara was breathing hard when she finally pulled away.

Thia rolled her eyes at her sister. "In front of us all, Kiara? Do you have to?"

Kiara grinned at Thia, happy to see her sister joking for once. "You're just jealous," she jibbed as she stepped away from Caedmon, her heart clenching as his warmth receded.

Kiara came to stand reluctantly beside Xyrisse and Thia. Her earlier reservations came flooding back in abundance.

Thia smiled encouragingly at her. Kiara closed her eyes. Her sister was right. Worries were a waste of time now. It was too late to back out of the plan and Kiara was still convinced that the *manach* could help them. Kiara finally nodded at Xyrisse.

Xyrisse smiled and held a hand out to both Kiara and Thia. "Focus on everything you remember of the *manach's* realm," Xyrisse instructed in her strange voice. "Picture yourself being there with them again."

Kiara nodded and closed her eyes, remembering the strange small people she had been with for an unreal time the previous winter. She breathed deeply and saw herself once again in their strange towers that looked so fragile and tiny from the outside but seemed fathomless from within.

Suddenly she was falling through time. "Keep the place we are going in your mind, Kiara." Xyrisse's voice floated from beyond reality.

Kiara continued to picture the bedchamber she had stayed in while with the *manach*, ignoring the spinning sensation that was carrying her though space. Flashing lights and bright colors pushed past her closed eyelids and a whirring sound filled her ears. And then there was silence.

Xyrisse dropped her hand and Kiara opened her eyes. And there they were in the ice tower of the *manach*, a dozen robed figures standing in a semi-circle in front of them.

"Kiara Carnesîr you have returned as we expected. Welcome."

CHAPTER TWENTY-FOUR

Mina watched Arion's face in the firelight. It was the 16th day since they'd abandoned her brother's camp and set off on their own and he still hadn't given her any hint as to why they had left Meldiron or where they were going. Mina had been trying to wait him out to see if he would fill her in on the details, as he'd promised to do when she agreed to go with him, but so far Arion had been silent on the matter.

In fact, he'd been silent on most things. He almost acted as if he were in mourning and Mina suspected that leaving Meldiron the way they had was the source of his pain. But what she couldn't understand was why Arion had insisted on leaving if it was going to hurt him so much. And it didn't look like he was going to enlighten her.

She knew they were travelling in a Westward direction. Arion had been almost too good at teaching her to navigate. By looking at the stars each night, she could tell approximately where they were and by her estimates, they were heading directly toward Séreméla.

It was odd that she didn't have any fears about what Arion was doing. Taking her and one of the only complete copies of the Prophecy back to Séreméla should have worried her but for some reason she didn't feel worried. She was annoyed that he hadn't shared with her what was going on but she still trusted Arion to take care of her with his life.

She'd been watching Arion for at least half an hour now and if he was aware of her scrutiny he was ignoring her. Mina's patience had come to an end.

"Arion, can you please tell me why we are heading directly toward Séreméla?" Mina asked quietly.

He looked at her in surprise.

"You shouldn't look so shocked, after all, you were the one who taught me to navigate," she pointed out drily. "You promised to tell me what was going on once we got far away from Meldiron," she paused and raised her eyebrows, "I don't think Meldiron is going to catch us."

Arion nodded and looked into the fire for a moment. Just when Mina thought he was going to ignore her, he began to speak. "I'm surprised that you've been patient for as long as you have," he noted wryly.

"I trust you," she said softly causing him to look at her face.

"I'm glad." He paused and seemed to be choosing his words carefully. "I've been trying to decide where to start. There is much to tell you."

"Why not start at the beginning?" Mina asked, "I find it is often the most useful place to start."

Arion inclined his head in agreement.

"Mina, you remember when Eöl Ar-Feiniel called you *Banphrionsa*?" he asked.

"Of course I do," Mina answered quietly, remember how she'd thought the old archivist's words to her were a form an endearment. She should have known better from an Elder.

"Meldiron told you that word meant Princess," he continued.

Mina nodded. That was the translation her brother had given her. Mina hadn't thought to question it.

"Well there is a deeper meaning to it. You were the Lost One. Banphrionsa, our treasured princess. If you noticed the Elder people being overly joyful to see you alive and well, there was a deeper reason than their kindness."

Mina thought back to her time in Sér"eméla. The Elders had been very welcoming to her. She remembered thinking they were such a friendly and happy race. Was Arion suggesting there was more to their enthusiasm?

"You see you were hidden away for a reason." He paused and then sighed. "Mina, when you learned the history of our people, did you ever notice how most of the leaders of the Elders were women?"

Mina thought back to the history books she had poured over with Eöl Ar-Feiniel. While she hadn't noticed it at the time, now that she thought of it she realized that Meldiron was correct. Most of the great leaders were females.

"In our tradition, the ruling monarchs are all female. However there are rules that specify the details of when our royal females can rule." Arion paused and looked at her intently.

Mina's stomach began to churn nervously. She had a feeling that she wasn't going to like what Arion had to tell her.

After a moment he spoke again. "The Elders ways are complex and difficult to understand. The tradition holds that female children born to the royal leader rule. But there are very few female children born into ruling families. No one knows why but it has always been the case. Remember your father was the son of a king. And his father also a son. In fact, you have to go back 12 generations before you can find a female ruler."

Mina nodded, remembering reading of the great Aibhilín who had ruled the Elders so many centuries ago.

"Female rulers are considered a great blessing." Arion smiled. "But they are also subject to certain rules."

Mina raised her eyebrows. She did not remember reading that part.

Arion ran his hand over his face and sighed as if he had a great burden to share with her. Mina's misgivings grew. She wasn't sure she actually wanted to hear what he had to tell her. But it was too late to go back to innocence. Arion's pale eyes were serious as he met hers again.

"As the first female born into the royal family in more than 500 years, you are a gift and a blessing to the Elder people," he told her.

Arion shook his head solemnly. "But Meldiron is the Crown Prince," she protested, rejecting what he was telling her.

"Meldiron was only the fall back ruler and he always knew that you were alive and well, even if our people did not. And so did the Elder council. Meldiron was simply taking care of our people until your return. He was never meant to be the ruler. And he always knew this."

Mina shook her head, unable to believe they would keep such a secret from her. "No," she whispered vehemently. She didn't want to rule anyone!

"Mina, deep down I think you know this is the truth," Arion told her.

She swallowed painfully, trying to process what he was telling her. She was the rightful ruler of the Elder people? It seemed fantastical and unbelievable.

And if it were true … terrifying!

And yet Arion looked completely serious. This was not a bad joke. Mina knew that he was speaking the truth.

"What if I don't want to be ruler?" Mina asked. "Can't I abdicate my throne to Meldiron?"

Arion shook his head, sadly. "No, Minathrial, this is your destiny. You are the chosen one. The Elder people have many hopes for their next female leader. You are the first in one so very long and now they know you are alive you will have to return and face up to your duty sooner or later."

Mina felt panic start to creep up her throat. "What if I don't want to?"

"Your wants do not come into it," Arion said firmly.

Mina looked at him, the panic threatening to choke her. She knew nothing about the Elder people, nothing about the tradition, nothing about what was expected of her. How could she possibly rule?

Arion was watching her sympathetically. "Mina, I know this is shocking for you. But you are the first female ruler born in so long and the only Marked One. You have the power to make a great difference in the Elder kingdom. The power to change the destiny of our people. And you will do well."

Arion sounded far more confident than she felt. How could she rule a people as powerful as the Elders? Mina was a simple village girl. Where would she learn how to do that? And from what she could see the Elder council was completely corrupted. How would she know who to trust and who not to?

"Where are we going, Arion?" she asked, suddenly wanting to be heading anywhere except to Séreméla.

"I think you know where we are going, Princess," he said gently.

"No!" she couldn't help it from slipping through her lips.

"Listen to reason." Arion said firmly. "The Elder people need you more than ever, Minathrial. You are the only chance for them to overcome the disease that is filling their minds, fed by the current Council, about the Marked Ones. If the Elder community supports the Marked children then we stand a chance of protecting them."

Suddenly she thought of her brother. If he knew that she was the Chosen One, then why did they have to sneak out of camp?

"What about Meldiron?" she asked.

Arion closed his eyes. "Your brother knows that you are destined to rule but he refuses to believe the level of corruption in the Elder council. He still trusts his old advisers – which is understandable, they have been guiding him since he was a child. He doesn't doubt their loyalties."

"And you do?" Mina asked.

Arion nodded. "I know many of them are corrupt. The trick will be identifying which ones are loyal."

Mina stared at him. He was talking about taking her into a political nightmare and asking her to rule. Even with the support of the people, it was a tricky situation.

"Who are you loyal to?" Mina asked suddenly.

"I am your *Coimirceoir*, Mina. I am loyal to only you." He watched her face intently.

"What does that mean? *Coimirceoir?*"

"It means Guardian. Every female consort for the Elder kingdom has one appointed to her from birth." Arion smiled grimly. "I was an odd choice, with my disfigurement but your grandmother was insistent. She had the foresight and said I was the only one in our generation who could be your *Coimirceoir*."

Mina's mouth went dry. She forced herself to ask, "And what are the duties of the *Coimirceoir?*"

"To protect the monarch at all costs. I am truly your Guardian, Mina."

She stared at him, suddenly feeling inexplicitly hurt. He was sworn by her birth to protect her with his life. And that's what he would do. She wasn't his friend. He had no feelings for her beyond his duty.

"Meldiron knew this?" she asked dully.

"Of course."

"Then why was he so angry at the riverbank when you ..." Mina trailed off, unable to finish the sentence.

"When I kissed you?" Arion closed his eyes painfully. "I forget that you are such a novice in the Elder ways. Mina, the Chosen One can't marry or have children. Instead the royal line continues through her eldest sibling, in this case Meldiron."

Mina stared at him.

"I knew by letting Meldiron believe that I, your *Coimirceoir*, had become romantically involved with you, he would banish me. It was the only way that I could ensure that he forced me to leave thereby opening the door to get you back to *Séreméla*."

"I can't have children or a family?" Mina asked weakly.

"I'm sorry, Princess. That is the duty of the Chosen One." Arion stood and gestured toward her tent. "You've had a lot to process and we must be on the road early tomorrow. We can talk more and when we arrive in *Séreméla* there are those who can tell you more about your duties as Queen. For now I think that you should rest."

Mina looked at him incredulously, wondering how he thought she would sleep with such shocking information dropped in her lap. He seemed to think she would just accept that her whole future was planned for her. But then again for Arion none of this was new. He had known for almost 17 years that she was the Chosen One and that he would be her *Coimirceoir*. He had been raised with such knowledge and to him it was the truth.

But this was *not* Mina's truth. She refused to believe that her life was so predetermined by destiny and tradition – a destiny and tradition that felt completely foreign to her.

Without saying another word, she rose from her place by the fire and went to her bedroll. She needed to keep her wits about her and think about all that Arion had told her. She needed to stay calm if she was going to come up with a plan for changing her destiny.

CHAPTER TWENTY-FIVE

Thia stared at the creatures in front of her as she tried to regain her equilibrium. Teleporting had been unsettling but she didn't have time to dwell on that now. As the strange beings moved closer, Thia gasped. From a distance one might mistake them for children they were so small. But they were far from youthful. Each one was wizen with dozens of wrinkles framing their small faces. And their eyes were wise beyond years.

Thia had the distinct impression that when they looked at her they knew everything about her.

"We know why you are here," one of them spoke as if reading her thoughts. "Come. The form of transport used by Xyrisse is tiring and unsafe for ones such as you." The small creature who was speaking stepped forward, reaching for Thia. Without thinking Thia stepped away.

"You have nothing to fear here, Thia. We are able to give you the help you seek but first you must sleep." Thia shook her head. Something felt wrong about this place. Out of the corner of her eye she saw Kiara and Xyrisse each leaving accompanied by a *manach*, unquestioningly. She resisted the urge to call to them and tell them to stay; to not be so trusting of these unknown creatures. Panic began to well within her as she watched her companions disappear.

"Come," the voice seemed to fill her head and as the creature reached for her, she suddenly was engulfed in the purple haze that warned of a seizure. Thia struggled to breathe to fight the sensation but she was falling into a vision.

A sick and unconscious Teague with Celeste at a strange entrance to the Underground with the sea boiling below them. Thia being pushed away by Celeste. Teague surrounded by the children of the People laughing and happy. Teague in the arms of an Underground girl, looking like his old self.

Thia pushed against the vision not wanting to see this but she was pulled under again. The scene shifted and suddenly a new vision took over.

Mina crying in Séreméla, Arion standing in the shadows behind her, a room full of Elders who were angrily yelling, Mina and Arion running through a desolate landscape.

Thia sobbed and struggled to surface but once again she dragged into a series of visions. On and on it went, vision of Caedmon and Kiara, Teague, Xyrisse, people she loved and knew and others she didn't know at all. And try as she might Thia couldn't break away from them. She was forced to watch as life event after life event flashed through her mind.

#

Even though she'd visited the *manach* before with Caedmon, Kiara was uneasy. She remembered so little from her last trip. It was just a hazy memory. She could attribute some of that to the fact that she had been recovering from the ice monster attack but not all of it. It was almost as if some of that experience had been washed from her mind until it was just a distant memory. She did remember that even when she had been here before, it had a strange surreal quality to it. Time had passed in a vacuum and both her and Caedmon had been surprised when they'd left the *manach* and found that the beginnings of spring had started in the Five Corners.

Before she'd left the Refuge, Caedmon had warned her to be careful. She thought he'd been referring to Xyrisse but now she wondered if he'd been referring to the little people. She wished she'd had more time with him so that she could ask him what he remembered from their last trip here. But it was too late now. She would just have to rely on her instincts and approach everything with a sense of caution.

That was hard to do with the *manach*, however. Already she was beginning to feel relaxed and at ease. She remembered the feeling of intense wellbeing that infused her last time she'd stayed with the little people. She suspected the *manach* were influencing her emotions.

"We knew you would return."

A small creature was suddenly standing in front of her. Kiara stared at it but didn't reply.

"You've done much good with the small ones, Kiara, but there is much danger ahead for all of you. You must be cautious as to whom you trust."

"How do I know I can trust you?" Kiara demanded suddenly, her suspicions tweaked. Her voice was loud in the quietude that infused the *manach* dwellings.

The small creature cocked its wizen head and smiled at her, its face creasing into even more folds. "You don't. And you shouldn't." It nodded. "We will give advice but it is you who must decide if you will follow it. It is good to be suspicious of even us. We encourage you to question everything."

Kiara narrowed her eyes. She couldn't shake the feeling that she was being manipulated. But she couldn't pinpoint how exactly.

"The Prophecy is strong. You must at least try to understand it," the *manach* continued.

"But we don't have it," Kiara interrupted. The only complete copy any of them had seen of the Prophecy had been stolen from Mina's desk in Séreméla before they left the Elder homeland. Meldiron said that Arion and Mina had found another complete copy but they had taken it with them when they fled the camp together. No one was clear on what their motives were.

The *manach* nodded. "You will need to find it and understand it if you have any hope of surviving against them," it told her. "Your sister Elder will be important in understanding."

Mina! "But I don't know where she is!" Kiara cried out.

"She is safe. As long as she is with her *Coimirceoir* she will be well. You must fear those who might try to separate them."

"Her what?" Kiara asked, not comprehending the words the *manach* was using.

"You are in grave danger from others," it continued as if it hadn't heard her question.

"From whom?" Kiara asked.

"The ones who would destroy you and all Marked Ones."

Kiara's brow furrowed, her patience wearing thin. The creature was speaking in circles and not telling her anything.

"How do we know who is a threat if you don't tell us."

"You mustn't give up," was all the *manach* would say.

Kiara took a deep breath and held it, counting to ten. This conversation was beyond frustrating.

Then the tiny *manach* put her wrinkled hand on Kiara's arm, her grasp surprisingly strong. "You, yourself, are about to face great peril, Kiara. They know you are one of the most dangerous ones."

Kiara pulled her arm away annoyed but the *manach* grabbed her again and squeezed until it hurt. "Listen to me. You must be careful. They will take you otherwise."

"What do you mean?" Kiara asked her heart suddenly beating. "Who will take me?"

But just then a second *manach* entered the room and the small one grasping her arm, let go. The conversation was over.

#

Xyrisse looked at the small creatures surrounding her. Their excited chatter filled her senses - not just her ears but her entire being.

She smiled tentatively at them. They were so different than anything she'd ever seen before. And they seemed to be intrigued by her.

One of them stepped forward and the others fell silent.

"Forgive us, young one. It has been a long time since we've seen a Nasseen in person. You are welcome here, Princess Xyrisse."

Xyrisse started. How had they known? She had kept her secret since Thia had found her, guarding it carefully so no one would suspect her true identity. Yet these creatures seemed to be truth-knowers.

"Relax, my dear, your secret is safe with us but you know you can't stay in hiding. Your father has already sent multiple groups of Hunters to the Five Corners. They won't stop until they have found you."

Xyrisse swallowed as her fear leapt into her throat. Her father's guards were the most deadly of all Hunters.

"If they find you with your friends, they will kill them all and take you back." The creature paused and smiled. "But you must know that."

Xyrisse found herself nodding without realizing it. Her thoughts immediately went to Meldiron who had been so kind to her. She didn't want to imagine what the Hunters would do to him if they found them together.

"You have the power to deal with this yourself," the wizen one went on.

Xyrisse shook her head. "I won't return," she said, fear clutching at her heart.

The small creature smiled at her sympathetically. "We both know that is not true. You must return and you will. It is preordained."

Xyrisse closed her eyes. The last thing she wanted was to return to her homeland. She had never felt such happiness or freedom as what she had felt since arriving in the Five Corners. And now they were suggesting she return of her own freewill.

Then the *manach* said something that surprised her, "You must take the Elder with you. He has an important role to play in Nasseet."

Xyrisse opened her eyes and stared at the *manach*. What role could Meldiron play in her homeland? The Nasseet people would not take kindly to an Elder. They didn't trust foreigners easily and in old times had closed their borders completely. But in her grandfather and father's rule, the borders had reopened as they had realized the advantage to having a rich trading relationship with the Five Corners. But still, an Elder, especially an Elder prince, like Meldiron, would not be welcomed with open arms.

"You are the future," the *manach* told her and then the group of them left her alone in her chamber.

#

When Thia finally woke she was in a dark room with small creatures all around her. Her head ached and the visions that had assaulted her were still chasing one another through her mind.

"Little One, you are well," a strangely familiar voice assured her. "You need to rest."

"I need to help Teague," Thia surprised herself by saying, her voice raspy and raw.

"You know what he needs."

Thia looked at the creatures around her unsure what they were saying and yet …

"Celeste …" Thia whispered.

"Yes. We know what you seek. The entrance to the Heartland."

"The Heartland?" Thia asked weakly.

"You know it as the Underground."

"Can you help me?"

"We can."

And for the first time in a long time, Thia felt hope. Then sleep reclaimed her.

CHAPTER TWENTY-SIX

The return trip to the Refuge was delayed slightly because of Thia's extreme reaction to the teleporting. The *manach* had explained that Thia's seizures, which had lasted two hours, had not been prompted by the *manach* themselves but by teleporting without proper preparation.

The *manach* were never critical of them but they were concerned by the fact that Thia had not been properly prepared for the teleport. They explained that if she had not ended up with them, she might have been stuck in a neverending seizure that would have eventually taken her life.

Not wanting to spark another serious episode, Xyrisse refused to teleport them until the *manach* had treated Thia with herbal medicines that would prevent such an attack. Thia, desperate to get back to Teague and initiate the plan that the *manach* had discussed with her, took the herbs without so much as a twinge of complaint.

She tried not to think about the onslaught of visions she had experienced. They were still too overwhelming to consider. And the ones concerning Teague, while positive, still stung her heart.

Thia couldn't help feeling a sense of foreboding when it came to Teague. The *manach* had been clear about one thing. Teague's only hope of recovery was to get him to Celeste. Her vision had shown him happy with children and a girl from the Underground. Thia wondered if wasn't a vision of how his life would play out if he did get help from Celeste. Would Teague make a life for himself with the People? Thia felt a strong sense of loss at the mere thought of it.

She wanted Teague to recover, of course, but the thought of losing him was unbearable. Sadness engulfed her. It seemed that Teague and her were destined to never have time together. Still if the alternative was only his death, Thia would have to let him go. She couldn't bear to imagine a world without Teague in it, even if it meant that he would be in it without her.

The *manach* had told Thia of an entrance to the Underground in the far Northeast of the Five Corners. It was beyond the Eastern Mountains. Thia didn't know anyone who had been to that part of the Five

Corners and the *manach* had determined that teleporting there would be dangerous. Xyrisse needed to have at least one person who had a clear view of where she was taking them for the teleporting to be safe.

Xyrisse, herself, seemed preoccupied since they'd arrived. She still would smile and answer Thia's questions but her friendly manner of the previous month had almost disappeared. When she thought Thia wasn't looking, Xyrisse seemed puzzled. Thia wondered what mysteries the *manach* had planted in the Nasseet girl's mind.

Kiara, as usual was impatient to return home. She wanted to see Caedmon, she said but Thia wondered if there was something more to her reluctance to stay any longer with the *manach*. She seemed even more edgy and irritable than normal. And when the *manach* finally gave their consent for Thia to travel, Kiara wouldn't wait another minute to leave.

"Let's go, Xyrisse, we've wasted enough time," Kiara said bluntly.

Xyrisse, to Thia's surprise, seemed just as eager as Kiara to leave the *manach*.

"Remember what we have told you," the smallest, most wizen of the creatures said as they linked hands and prepared for the transport.

Thia's last conscious thought was to wonder whether they had all been told different things.

#

Caedmon was waiting for them when they arrived in the same spot they had teleported from to begin with. Kiara wondered how he had known that they would return at that precise moment. There really had been no way for them to communicate with him while they were with the *manach*. Kiara wondered if he had been waiting for them the entire time they were gone. It didn't seem realistic but his being there was too coincidental.

"How did you know we were coming?" Kiara demanded, pushing down the immediate joy she felt when she saw him.

"Teague," Caedmon said darkly. "He was raving most of the night saying Thia was in danger." Caedmon looked at her sister. "Were you?"

Thia shook her head.

"She wasn't in danger at all," Kiara said. "The *manach* made sure she'd been given herbs to protect her from the teleporting."

"Is he worse?" Thia asked quietly.

Caedmon pressed his lips together and averted his gaze. After a moment he gave a swift nod.

"But more importantly, did the *manach* know how to help?" He asked.

Thia stepped forward and put her small hand on Caedmon's inked forearm. "They did," she said softly. "They agreed that Celeste would be the best chance of his recovery. And they told us where the closest entrance to the Underground is."

He looked down at Thia. Kiara could see him fighting against the hope that her words were bringing him.

She spoke, "It won't be easy."

Caedmon looked at her, hope fast fading from his dark eyes.

"Where?" he asked finally.

"Beyond the Dark Hill Mountains on the cliffs overlooking the East Sea," Thia answered before Kiara could. "There is an entrance halfway down the sheerest cliff."

Caedmon swore under his breath. "And how are we to get Teague in his current condition there? He can't teleport. How are we realistically supposed to undertake such a journey?"

"He can do it," Thia said firmly. "I can work with him. And I have the herbs that can sedate him safely if he gets too agitated."

Kiara looked at her sister in surprise.

"The *manach* gave them to me," Thia muttered apologetically.

"Don't apologize," Kiara said. "The easier we can make this journey the better. When do we leave?"

Xyrisse stepped forward suddenly. Kiara had forgotten she was there. "Don't you think we should speak to Meldiron and the others before we make the plans?" she asked hesitantly. "There are considerations for everyone involved and how we proceed affects not just Teague but all of us." She looked at them each in turn, her red eyes serious. "You know how removing Teague from the Refuge will be received by Bellasiel."

Kiara stopped herself from rolling her eyes. Bellasiel would be furious to lose Teague. Despite the fact that she insisted he be kept locked in a dungeon, it was clear that he was very important to the Elder and her plans for the Refuge. But Xyrisse was right. If they took Teague from her, Bellasiel would not likely be welcoming upon their return.

"We need a plan."

Xyrisse nodded.

Caedmon straightened. "Find the others and tell them we'll meet in my quarters in an hour."

#

They were assembled in less than an hour. From the looks on their faces, Mina could tell that everyone was feeling just as tense as she was. They had left Teague in the dungeon, not wanting to draw attention to themselves or to upset him.

"So the question is how do we get Teague out of the Refuge?" Meldiron asked quietly after hearing what the girls had discovered with the *manach*.

Caedmon nodded. "Bellasiel is not going to just let him go. I think we can agree on that."

Kiara stood up and began pacing. "I say we take the children and all leave."

"That's not possible," Meldiron said irritably.

Kiara whirled and glared at him. "How do you know? We haven't even discussed the option."

Meldiron stood up and strode across the room, his stance just as aggressive as Kiara's. "Because I think before I speak," he said roughly. "Do you think that Bellasiel planned this place herself? She had been able to recruit over 100 Marked Ones and bring them here. And for some reason it appears to be a safe place for them."

"He is right," Xyrisse interjected. "With the number of Hunters scouring the Five Corners, these children should be easy to sniff out and yet … they are safe here."

"You call being trained to be soldier safe?" Kiara cried in disgust.

"Safer than the alternative," Meldiron reminded her and they fell silent, remembering the countless dead children with the Mark.

"So we agree that moving the children is not viable at this point," Caedmon noted. "But Teague needs to get to the Underground and the only safe entrance is to the East Sea."

The room was filled with sounds of assent.

"Thia must come with Teague because she knows this Celeste person and also knows where the entrance is based on what the *manach* have told her."

Again they agreed.

"I will go with Teague for obvious reasons beyond the fact that he's my brother." Caedmon paused and suddenly looked at Kiara. Thia sensed he was going to say something her sister would not like. "Kiara, I think you should stay here."

Thia closed her eyes and waited for Kiara's predictable outburst.

"What?" Kiara opened her mouth to continue but Caedmon cut her off.

"You can protect the children. They trust you - more than any of the rest of us. After all you are the one who saved them." He walked over to her and put his hands on her shoulders until she met his eyes. "You are responsible for them now."

Kiara closed her mouth and to Thia's surprise she didn't argue. Instead her eyes filled with tears.

Caedmon bent his head and kissed her then murmured something none of them could hear. Kiara nodded. Thia suddenly had the uncomfortable feeling that she was intruding on a private moment. After a time, Caedmon stepped back and turned to them.

"I think it would be best if our party remained small. The rest of you should stay here, planning for our next move."

"I will not be staying." It was Xyrisse who spoke. Thia stared at her in surprise but it was Meldiron who answered her.

"Don't be ridiculous," he said with a laugh.

But Xyrisse was clearly serious.

"Meldiron, I am sorry." She closed her eyes but Mina could see pink tinged tears streaking down her cheeks. "I have lied to you." Xyrisse paused and took a deep breath. "To all of you."

Kiara reached for her dagger. "I knew it." She moved to stepped forward but Meldiron blocked her way.

"Don't."

Thia found words leaving her own mouth. "Xyrisse, what do you mean that you lied?"

She turned to Thia, the pain raw on her face. "Forgive me, Thia. I had no choice. I was desperate." She turned back to the Elder. "I am sorry, Prince Meldiron. I did lie to you. But I meant no harm."

Kiara glared at her but Thia stepped forward and touched Xyrisse's arm.

"How did you lie?" she pressed softly.

Xyrisse turned back to Meldiron before she answered. Thia watched as the Elder nodded to her. "It's okay," he said softly.

"I must return to my homeland," Xyrisse said instead of answering the question.

"What?" Meldiron asked, disbelief staining his words. "You can't go back - they will kill you!"

Xyrisse looked sad. "No. Meldiron. No, they will not kill me. That is where I lied."

Thia watched him as confusion filled his handsome features. She felt a pang of pity for him. She was just as confused as he was.

"I ran away. They did not dump me in the dunes," Xyrisse said softly.

"Then you're not a Hunter?"

"Oh, no. That part was true. And they did kill my brother. I was one of a handful of the Nasseet of my generation who was gifted with the ability to Hunt. Gifted or cursed." She swallowed and paused. "But what I didn't tell you was that I was …" She paused again then met Meldiron's eye. "I am the Princess of Nasseet."

CHAPTER TWENTY-SEVEN

Xyrisse sat in her chamber gathering up the last of her courage. Returning to Nasseet would not be easy but she could see no way around it. The *manach* had made it clear that what she feared was true. The Hunters had been unleashed by her father and would not stop until they found her. And they would ruthlessly destroy anything that got in their way. The thought that her new friends might be hurt because of her was too much.

The return trip home would be easy. She just had to prepare herself to teleport. But she was stalling. She knew it. She had to say goodbye to Meldiron before she left. She had already given her farewells to Thia but she felt she owed something a bit more to the Elder prince.

And if she were honest she would admit that she didn't really want to bid him farewell. Xyrisse couldn't deny that she found the tall, handsome Elder prince attractive. Anyone would. But that wasn't why she was drawn to him. He treated her like she was a normal person, which was rare in the Five Corners. Everywhere Xyrisse had gone in this land, people had physically recoiled from her. Only Meldiron and Thia treated her like she was a real person. The others either treated her with distrust or looked at her like she was a monster.

Xyrisse had to admit that it had been nice to have a friend for once in her life. Back in Nasseet, as both a Hunter and royalty, her only friend had been her little brother, Telekles. His murder had been more than just a killing of a sibling but the killing of her closest confidant. The fact that her father had approved the murder just made it that much more painful. Xyrisse had fled her homeland right after it happened.

Pushing those thoughts aside, she rose and made her way through the Refuge to Meldiron's chambers. There was no point in putting off her farewells. Standing in the hall outside his door she hesitated once again. Perhaps it would be better for her to just leave. But she just couldn't bring herself to do that.

Before she could change her mind, Xyrisse's knocked on the door.

Almost immediately it swung open and she found herself face to face with the Elder prince.

"I ..." Xyrisse shook her head, starting to turn away.

"Xyrisse wait!" Meldiron pushed the door open "Please, come in," he said gently.

Hesitating a moment, Xyrisse stepped over the threshold.

"I don't mean to interrupt. I just wanted to say goodbye," she said as she turned to face Meldiron, her words dying on her lips when she saw the expression in his forest green eyes. Pain, sadness and behind that a deep longing.

"You aren't interrupting," he assured her. "Please stay for a few moments." He gestured to the chair beside him.

Xyrisse sat and looked at Meldiron, trying to ignore the way her heart quickened just a little.

"Caedmon and Thia will be leaving soon to take Teague to the Underground. Kiara will stay and work with the Marked Ones, watching over them." Meldiron paused then went on. "But that leaves the two of us."

Xyrisse nodded, wondering what they had decided he would do. She didn't expect what he said next.

"I would like to accompany you back to Nasseet."

Xyrisse was so surprised she didn't know what to say. She remembered the words of the *manach* telling her that she had to take Meldiron with her. But she didn't want to imagine how the presence of an Elder would be received in her homeland.

"I can't let you risk that," she said softly.

"Xyrisse, I want to come," Meldiron insisted. "Call it strange but I've had a deep desire to visit Nasseet since we were in Sailsburg. You can ask Thia if you don't believe me." He paused before adding, "If you don't take me, I will make my way back to the port city and stow away on a boat. That was my first plan."

Xyrisse gasped in shock. "Stowing away is not something to joke about," she scolded, "It would guarantee a swift death for you."

Meldiron raised his eyebrows, "Well, I guess you will have to take me with you then," he teased.

Xyrisse shook her head. "You are an unfair bargainer, Prince Meldiron!"

He laughed. "But you'll take me?"

Xyrisse bit her lip. She shouldn't agree to this but before he could ask her again she found herself saying, "Yes, I will take you to Nasseet."

CHAPTER TWENTY-EIGHT

By the time Bellasiel discovered that not only had Caedmon and Thia had taken Teague, but that Meldiron had left with Xyrisse, too, it was too late for her to do more than show her rage to Kiara.

Kiara wasn't too concerned. Bellasiel could growl but she didn't think she would throw Kiara in a dungeon like she had done with Teague. Kiara was important to the children at the Refuge and Bellasiel would do anything to keep those children happy and under her control. And as much as Kiara hated to admit it, it was true that the Refuge was the only safe haven for the Marked Children at present.

She started to train the children in the mornings and worked on keeping up her own training in the afternoons. Often groups of children would come and watch her as she trained. Kiara was patient and answered their questions, trying to ease their loneliness and at the same time keep her own mind free from worry about her sisters and Caedmon.

She wasn't happy about being the one left behind but she did understand Caedmon's reasoning. For reasons she couldn't explain she wasn't worried about Mina. She felt that her sister was where she was meant to be with Arion. And honestly, Kiara truly believed that as far away from the Refuge as Mina could get would be safer for her.

It was six weeks after the parties had departed that Bellasiel came to see her. The Elder had calmed down about what she saw as the betrayal by Caedmon and Thia. She had questioned Kiara on numerous occasions but Kiara had remained firm in her denial of knowing where they had gone. At first Bellasiel's rage was so vivid Kiara feared the Elder might resort to torture to get her to talk. But as time went on, it became apparent that she didn't believe that Kiara knew where they had gone. Or she didn't care anymore, although Kiara found that hard to believe.

Lately Bellasiel had taken to coming to the training sessions to watch Kiara work with the children. What she saw seemed to please her. The Elder was warmer to Kiara than she had been in months.

One afternoon Bellasiel came to Kiara's chambers unannounced.

"Kiara I appreciate that you are the only chosen Marked One who has not deserted us," Bellasiel began, her pale eyes icy.

Kiara waited silently and couldn't help wondering where this conversation was going.

"You know how disappointed we were when the others left." The Elder paused. "But you've shown you are loyal. And I feel I can trust you."

Kiara didn't believe a word of what Bellasiel was saying but she kept her face passive, waiting to hear what the Elder leader was going to reveal. Sometimes one could learn a lot from listening to another's lies.

"You know that the Hunters' presence in Five Corners peaked in the fall last year." Kiara nodded, wondering if Bellasiel knew that it was Xyrisse's presence that had sparked the increase in Hunting activity. She had not been pleased to find the Nasseet girl with them when they arrived at the Refuge but Meldiron had spoken to her privately and she had let Xyrisse stay. Kiara was sure Bellasiel was regretting that decision.

"Our sources now say that the Hunters have almost disappeared from Five Corners in the last 3 weeks," Bellasiel said her eyes on Kiara. "Surprising?"

Kiara knew that Xyrisse and Meldiron must have made it to the Island of Nasseet if the Hunters had disappeared. She hoped the Meldiron was safe. Going to an island wholly infested with the Nasseet assassins did not appeal to her. But she kept her face passive. "Very surprising," she said quietly.

Bellasiel's eyes narrowed slightly. Then she forced a smile to her thin lips. "It is good news though. I'm sure you will be more excited that most of us."

Kiara looked at the Elder sharply. "What do you mean?" she asked cautiously.

Bellasiel laughed, the sound brittle and sharp like broken glass. "Well, Kiara, you can start saving Marked Children again. You've not brought any new ones to the Refuge since last fall. You must feel that you are failing those children who remain in the Five Corners."

Kiara paused unsure what to say. She was positive that any way she answered was going to get her in trouble.

"It is rather dangerous for me to seek the children on my own, don't you think?" she asked carefully.

Bellasiel shook her head. "Is that what Caedmon would have you believe? I know for a fact that it was you who save most of the children."

Bellasiel paused. "And I've seen you training. You are more than capable of taking care of yourself."

She was watching Kiara closely. After a few tense moments she handed a sheaf of papers to her. "We have received a plea from parents in three different towns to get help for their children. You are still committed to saving them, aren't you, Kiara?"

Sensing that Bellasiel wanted her to be gone from the Refuge for some reason, Kiara raked her mind for an excuse to stay. And she came up blank. Given how passionate she'd been in finding the Marked Children the previous summer and fall, there was no reason she could come up with that would seem believable to Bellasiel. Particularly when they had direct requests from parents.

Finally she just nodded.

"Good. Then you'll leave tomorrow at first light. We'll expect you and at least three Marked Ones to return within a week." Bellasiel stood.

Kiara walked her to the door silently. She studied the files Bellasiel had given her. They seemed legitimate. And Bellasiel was right, none of the children were too far from the Refuge.

Kiara remembered the dead children she'd found on her many scouting trips last summer. How she'd wished she could help them. And she thought of all the children who must have been killed since they'd quit going on their rescue missions.

While she still didn't approve of Bellasiel training the Marked children into tiny soldiers, it was still better than letting them die at the hands of Hunters, wasn't it?

Putting the papers on her desk, she turned to her closet and began stuffing a few things into a small bag. She would save as many Marked Ones as she could.

#

The next day Kiara found herself in a dense forest. She was beyond frustrated. She had left the Refuge at first light, just as Bellasiel had suggested but the first village she arrived in didn't have any record of the family of the first child that had been in Bellasiel's papers. In fact, there was no sign of any Marked children living in that village.

The second village she was to go to was not on the map. Instead there was a dark dense forest.

Kiara, a natural hunter, was used to forests and the wild animals that lived in them but there was something sinister about the forest she'd found herself in this afternoon.

Her doubts about Bellasiel returned. And for the first time she began to wonder if this wasn't some kind of trap.

The thought had barely been formed when five large dark figures emerged from the woods to surround her. Taking up a fighter's stance, Kiara pulled her sword from its scabbard but before she could engage any of her attackers, a larger figure approached. It said something in a tongue she didn't recognize and then she felt the sting of something in her right shoulder. She barely processed the fact that she had been struck by a dart of some kind before she felt the darkness overcoming her.

Her last thought was of Caedmon. He would never find her.

<<<<>>>

THE END

LIST OF NAMES AND PLACES

Characters

Minathrial (Min-ath-ree-al) called "Mina" (Meen-ah) – Sister to Thia and Kiara.

Elethia (E-leth-ee-ah) called "Thia" (Thee-ah) – Sister to Mina and Kiara

Kiara (Key-Ar-Ah)– Sister to Mina and Thia

Brijit (Bri-jeet)– Adopted mother of Mina, Thia and Kiara

Caedmon (C-ay-d-mon) – Brother to Teague

Teague (Tee-gue) – Brother to Caedmon

Arion (Air-ee-on) – Elder

Meldiron (Mel-dear-on)– Elder

Bellasiel (Bella-seel)– Elder and Healer

Eöl Ar-Feiniel (Ay-owl Are-Fen-el) – Elder and Archivist

Xyrisse (Xy-ris-se)

Celeste (Suh-leste) – Undergrounder

Manach (Men-ack) – Monks

Coimirceoir (Coym-eer-see-oy-ri) – Protector of the Princess

Draíodóir (Dray-Or-Door) – Druid/Magician

Places

Séreméla (Sar-A-Mell-A) – the Elders' home

MAP OF FIVE CORNERS

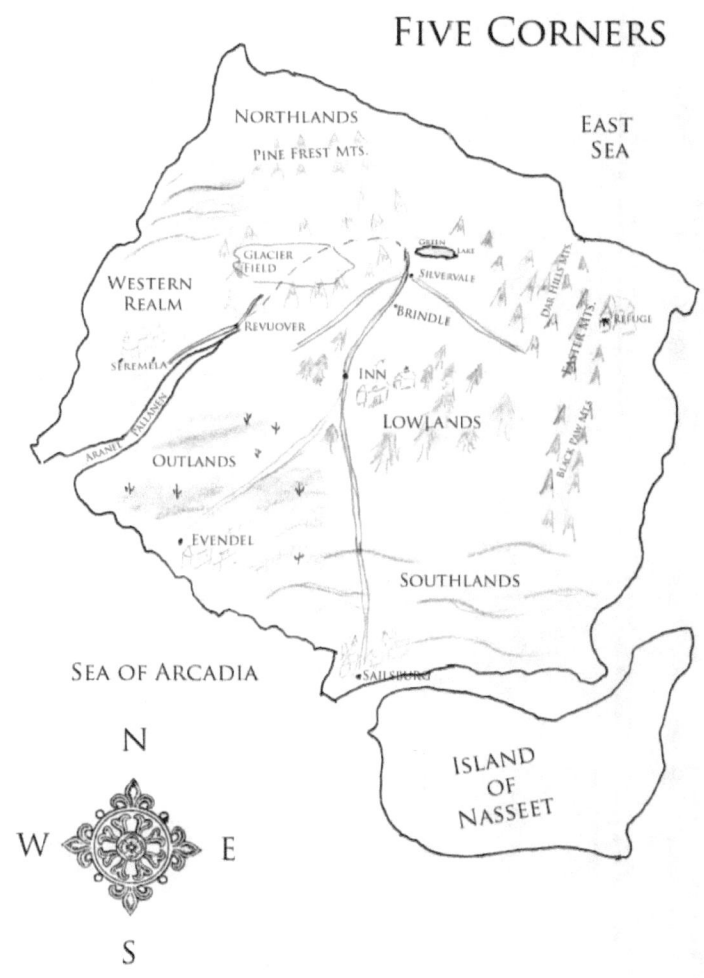

FIVE CORNERS

NORTHLANDS

PINE FREST MTS.

EAST SEA

GLACIER FIELD

GREEN LAKE

SILVERVALE

WESTERN REALM

REVUOVER

BRINDLE

OAK HILLS MTS.

EASTER MTS.

REFUGE

STREMELA

INN

LOWLANDS

BLACK EDGE MTS.

ARANEL FLELANDS

OUTLANDS

EVENDEL

SOUTHLANDS

SEA OF ARCADIA

SAILSBURG

N
W   E
S

ISLAND OF NASSEET

www.ingramcontent.com/pod-product-compliance
Lightning Source LLC
Chambersburg PA
CBHW020607250626
47154CB00004B/1401